OVERNEWTON CO

W9-AUX-640

+ 3965 092492 2

PRAISE FOR THE JACK MASON ADVENTURES

'A fun story, easy to read and full of action…
Bonus points for being the first kids' book of
its kind I've come across that gives mention
to the suffragettes!' *Books+Publishing*

'Lots of mechanical mayhem and derring-do—
breathless stuff.' Michael Pryor

'Non-stop action, non-stop adventure,
non-stop fun!' Richard Harland

'Set in a fantastical London, filled with airships,
steam cars and metrotowers stretching into space,
this fast-paced adventure and homage to the world
of Victorian literature and Conan Doyle offers an
enjoyable roller-coaster read for fans of *Artemis
Fowl* and the Lemony Snicket series…[a] rollicking
who-dunnit that will keep young Sherlocks
guessing to the very end.' *Magpies*

'Charming, witty and intelligently written…
This series no doubt will be a huge hit for early
teens, the writing is intelligent and Darrell Pitt
has created characters that challenge and provoke
readers to invest in the storyline.' Diva Booknerd

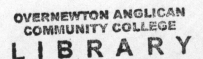

OVERNEWTON ANGLICAN
COMMUNITY COLLEGE
LIBRARY

THE JACK MASON ADVENTURES

Book I *The Firebird Mystery*
Book II *The Secret Abyss*
Book III *The Broken Sun*
Book IV *The Monster Within*
Book V *The Lost Sword*

DARRELL PITT began his lifelong appreciation of Victorian literature when he read the Sherlock Holmes stories as a child, quickly moving on to H. G. Wells and Jules Verne. This early reading led to a love of comics, science fiction and all things geeky. Darrell is now married with one daughter. He lives in Melbourne.

DARRELL PITT

The Lost Sword

A Jack Mason Adventure

TEXT PUBLISHING MELBOURNE AUSTRALIA

textpublishing.com.au

The Text Publishing Company
Swann House
22 William Street
Melbourne Victoria 3000
Australia

Copyright © Darrell Pitt 2015

The moral rights of Darrell Pitt have been asserted.

All rights reserved. Without limiting the rights under copyright above, no part of this publication shall be reproduced, stored in or introduced into a retrieval system, or transmitted in any form or by any means (electronic, mechanical, photocopying, recording or otherwise), without the prior permission of both the copyright owner and the publisher of this book.

First published in 2015 by The Text Publishing Company

Design by WH Chong
Cover illustration by Eamon O'Donoghue
Typeset by J&M Typesetting

Printed in Australia by Griffin Press, an Accredited ISO AS/NZS 14001:2004 Environmental Management System printer

National Library of Australia Cataloguing-in-Publication entry:
Author: Pitt, Darrell
Title: The lost sword / by Darrell Pitt.
ISBN: 9781925240184 (paperback)
ISBN: 9781925095982 (ebook)
Series: Pitt, Darrell Jack Mason adventures ; 5.
Target Audience: For young adults.
Subjects: Detective and mystery stories.
Dewey Number: A823.4

This book is printed on paper certified against the Forest Stewardship Council® Standards. Griffin Press holds FSC chain-of-custody certification SGS-COC-005088. FSC promotes environmentally responsible, socially beneficial and economically viable management of the world's forests.

THE LOST SWORD

CHAPTER ONE

That's strange, Jack Mason thought.

After entering the reception area of 221 Bee Street, he expected to see Gloria Scott, the blonde-haired secretary, at her desk. Instead the apartment was quiet.

The sitting room was also empty, apart from the addition of a backdrop from *Swan Lake*, a dozen busts of Napoleon and a life-size statue of a horse called *Silver Blaze*. These recent acquisitions had been jammed into the already crowded home, making it seem even more like a second-hand shop, instead of the residence of Ignatius Doyle, the famous detective.

Fifteen-year-old Jack Mason lived here with Scarlet Bell, a pretty redhead with a heart-shaped face. As assistants to Ignatius Doyle, they had travelled all over the world on several adventures, and were accustomed to strange events. When Jack had left the apartment to post some letters, Mr Doyle had been conducting one of his many odd experiments: trying to accurately fire a weapon while wearing a straitjacket, all the time being lowered into a vat of boiling oil.

As well as having an encyclopaedic mind and powers of observation, Mr Doyle was also the most eccentric man Jack had ever met.

Before he'd gone, Scarlet had been playing a record of some classical music—some chap named Mozart. There was no sign of her, either.

Where is everyone?

Jack checked the bedrooms, library and kitchen. He was passing the dining room when a tiny sound came from within. Pushing the door open, he blinked. The room was decorated with streamers, sparklers and hydrogen-filled balloons. In the middle of the table sat a cake with burning candles.

'*Surprise!*'

Jack almost fainted as a group of people leapt up from behind the table—Mr Doyle, Scarlet, his tutor Miss Bloxley, and Inspector Greystoke from Scotland Yard—and burst into a chorus of *Happy Birthday*.

Scarlet gave him a kiss on the cheek. 'Happy fifteenth birthday, Jack,' she said.

'Thank you,' Jack stammered. 'You all fooled me completely.'

He *had* been fooled, but he hadn't forgotten his birthday. That, and his parents, who had been tragically killed in a circus accident, had been on his mind for several days.

The last birthday gift they had given him was a copy of *Great Expectations* by Charles Dickens. It had gone missing when he was forced to leave the circus and live in the orphanage.

'There was a last-minute mishap,' Gloria said. 'Ignatius had some problems escaping the straitjacket.'

'I had to use some old-fashioned muscle to push the vat out of the way,' Miss Bloxley boomed. 'Ignatius was seconds away from turning into boiled chicken!'

'I'm not as fast as I once was,' Mr Doyle admitted.

'Even if you were only half the man,' Inspector Greystoke said, 'you'd still be the greatest asset that Scotland Yard has ever had.' He turned to Jack. 'Happy birthday, young fellow.'

'Thank you, sir,' Jack said. 'I appreciate you coming. You must have quite a busy schedule.'

'I do, but you and Scarlet have saved the day so many times that I had to show my appreciation.'

After the cake was eaten, and lemonade consumed, Jack was given his presents. Miss Bloxley and Inspector Greystoke gave him records—Jack had recently acquired a taste for jazz music—while the others gave him books.

'Ah,' Jack said, reading the title of Miss Bloxley's book. '*The History of Rome.*'

'I know you have an interest in Roman History.'

'I do.' Jack searched his memory. '*Ipsa scientia potestas est.*'

Miss Bloxley looked impressed. '*Knowledge itself is power*. Well done. You have been studying your Latin.'

The book from Scarlet was an adventure novel. '*Brigadier Gerard*,' Jack said. 'Looks interesting.'

'The stories are both exciting and humorous,' she said. 'Almost as good as the Brinkie Buckeridge novels.'

'I'll take your word for it.' He studied the book from Mr Doyle, a leather-jacket volume filled with blank pages.

'It's a diary,' Mr Doyle explained. 'I thought it time you started writing down your incredible exploits.'

'Thank you, sir.'

The party continued until Miss Bloxley and Inspector Greystoke left. As Jack and the others washed the dishes, a *ding* came from reception. Gloria returned with a note in hand.

'It's from 10 Downing Street,' Mr Doyle read. 'The prime minister has asked us to go there immediately.'

Within minutes, Jack, Scarlet and Mr Doyle were passing over London in their airship, the *Lion's Mane*. The balloon of the thirty-foot airship was gold, with a brass and timber gondola beneath. A picture of a lion, with the registration number—*1887*—decorated the bow.

'I wonder what the prime minister wants,' Scarlet said. 'A new mystery would be good. I *have* been a little bored of late. The latest Brinkie Buckeridge novel was due out last month, but it's been held up by the printers' strike.'

'*Ninja Attack* has been held up too,' Jack said. It was the sequel to his current favourite book, *Ninety-Nine Ninjas*.

Scarlet groaned. 'Not again,' she said. 'There are no such things as ninjas, Jack! Not these days.'

'Just because you haven't seen something doesn't mean it doesn't exist.'

From the corner, Mr Doyle harrumphed. *He* needed evidence.

Jack peered over the side of the airship. It was early autumn and the leaves were just beginning to turn. A row of buildings was being demolished on one side of the street, reducing the traffic to a single lane.

Jack's eyes moved to airships crisscrossing the horizon, and the London Metrotower, a building that stretched all the way to the edge of space.

After they'd landed at Downing Street, Jack felt a little self-conscious. He was still wearing his usual brown pants, a white shirt and his trademark green coat. Mr Doyle had dressed in a suit and bowler hat, and Scarlet a blue day dress.

'Maybe we should have changed,' Jack suggested.

'Never fear,' Mr Doyle said. 'I once visited the prime minister dressed as an emu.'

'Coming from you, Mr Doyle,' Scarlet said, 'that doesn't surprise me.'

They were shown into the office where they found Prime Minister Kitchener behind his desk. He was tall and stern-looking, but smiled when he shook hands with Jack and the others.

'Welcome back to Downing Street,' he said. 'It's been too long.'

To the side of the desk sat another man, smaller and rounder, with a face like a bulldog.

'General Churchill,' Mr Doyle greeted him. 'Still smoking those cigars?'

'I am indeed,' he confirmed. 'My doctor tells me they're bad for my health, but I'm not convinced.'

'I have my own blend for my pipe,' Mr Doyle said. 'It contains everything except tobacco.' As they took seats around the desk, he continued, 'Prime Minister, I assume you didn't invite us here for tea and scones.'

'Not exactly,' Kitchener said. 'There's a security matter we'd like to discuss with you that may impact the future peace and prosperity of our country.' He paused. 'No doubt you're aware of circumstances in Germany.'

'How could I not be?' Mr Doyle said, his face darkening. 'Those damned Nazis are gaining steam again. I'd hoped we'd seen the last of them.'

Jack swallowed. They had encountered the Nazis on his first adventure with Mr Doyle. During that time, the Nazis had seized power in Germany, but had just as quickly been deposed. A recent economic downturn had since helped them to become the country's third most powerful party—something that worried the British government.

'Their leader, Anton Drexler, has been sending diplomatic envoys to several countries,' Churchill said, 'with the intention of building stronger ties in the event of another war.'

'Another war?' Scarlet said. 'Surely there's no chance of that?'

'We hope not,' Kitchener said, 'but it's a possibility.'

'Some months ago, we were told the Nazis had sent agents to Japan,' Churchill continued. 'Their intention was to find a lost relic, a weapon known as the Kusanagi sword.'

'I've heard of it,' Mr Doyle said, nodding. 'Also known as the Grass Cutter Sword, it's reported to be over a thousand years old. It was supposedly used by a hero named Yamato Takeru to generate a mighty wind that repelled a grass fire and destroyed his enemies. The sword was lost in a shipwreck hundreds of years ago. It's all superstition, of course,' he added, sheepishly.

'Superstition, it may be,' Churchill said, 'but the Japanese government would be forever grateful to the man—and the nation—that recovered it for them.'

'Surely you don't expect me to find this sword?' Mr Doyle said. 'If it ever existed, it's probably lying at the bottom of the ocean. There must be someone else who can organise the search.'

'We did have another man,' Churchill admitted. 'He was making great progress until three days ago. Then he went missing.'

Mr Doyle shrugged. 'I'm sorry to hear that,' he said. 'But it's still not my area.'

General Churchill pursed his lips. 'I regret to inform you that the man who has gone missing is your brother.'

Brother? Jack sat forward. *I didn't know Mr Doyle had a brother.*

Scarlet looked just as surprised.

'My brother...' Mr Doyle's voice trailed off. 'You don't mean—'

'Edgar Doyle,' Kitchener confirmed. 'He is the man we sent to Japan in search of the Kusanagi sword.'

'Mr Doyle,' Jack said. 'You never told us you had a brother.'

'He is my *step*-brother,' Mr Doyle said, frowning. 'And a scoundrel. That is why I have never mentioned him.' He focused on Churchill. 'Which leaves me to ask why the British government sent him to find such a relic?'

'As you know,' Churchill said, 'Edgar spent some time in jail for a string of offences.'

'Edgar is a consummate thief,' Mr Doyle told Jack and Scarlet. 'His robberies include the theft of famous jewels, paintings and ancient artefacts from a dozen museums.'

'He was released from jail just prior to the start of the war,' Churchill explained. 'At that time, he approached us with an offer.'

'To be a spy?'

Churchill nodded. 'We needed someone who was adept at getting in and out of places. Edgar was most useful. At the end of the war we decided to continue his services in an unofficial capacity.'

'He's been doing jobs that could never be officially sanctioned by the government,' Kitchener said. 'We would deny all knowledge if he were caught.'

'And now he is missing,' Mr Doyle mused. 'I'm not the man for the job. I've been to Japan, but a local person would be better equipped—'

'The young lad who was helping your brother is extremely capable. He will give you any assistance you require.'

'Still—'

'Ignatius,' the prime minister said. 'We want the Kusanagi sword found and returned to the Japanese government. This is not a request.' His steely eyes focused on the detective, then softened. 'At the same time, you can find your brother.'

Mr Doyle swallowed. 'I'll do my best,' he said.

'As you always do.'

'And you already have a cover story for being in the country,' Churchill said. 'I understand you've been invited to be guest of honour at the annual International Darwinist Symposium.'

'I have. It's to be the largest meeting of Darwinist scientists in history, not to mention the diplomats from almost every country on earth.'

'Why is there so much interest this year?' Jack asked.

'The focus of this year's symposium is Hot Earth theory, a belief that the world is heating because of the burning of fossil fuels. The Darwinists are asking all scientists to ratify the Hot Earth Accord, demanding that fossil fuels be phased out.'

Jack wasn't sure he followed what Mr Doyle was

saying, but it sounded big.

'I was ready to decline their invitation,' Mr Doyle told Churchill. 'I was hoping to spend some time with my son.'

Long believed to have died in the war, Phillip Doyle had been found alive, but greatly affected by his experiences. Now on the mend, he had regular visits from Mr Doyle.

'I promise we'll make this up to you,' Kitchener promised.

Churchill paused at the front door as he led them out. 'I know you're not keen to go,' he said, 'but there's much at stake here. Britain may again be at war and we'll need all the allies we can gather.'

'I doubt we can find this mythical sword,' Mr Doyle warned, 'but we'll do what we can.'

Within minutes they were back on board the *Lion's Mane*, returning to Bee Street.

'You know what this means?' Jack said to Scarlet.

'What?'

'We'll be seeing some ninjas.'

'Jack,' Scarlet groaned. 'There are no such things as ninjas.'

'They were real in feudal Japan,' Mr Doyle said, from his position at the console. 'Unlike samurai warriors, who observed a strict code of conduct, ninjas acted as a kind of secret agent. Employed by princes or other powerful people, they would disguise themselves, carrying out acts of sabotage, assassination and espionage.'

'So there may still be some around,' Jack said.

'I doubt it. They have not existed for many years.'

Jack was disappointed, but not ready to give up hope. Ninjas were trained in the art of concealment. Surely their best defence was making people believe they didn't exist?

'Will we be taking the *Lion's Mane*?' Scarlet asked.

'No,' Mr Doyle replied. 'For this journey we'll use something a little bigger.'

CHAPTER TWO

'Bazookas,' Jack breathed. 'I'd forgotten the size of this thing.'

The London Metrotower was visible from all over the city, but it was rare to actually see it up close. Curving gently, it shot through the clouds and disappeared into the ether like a giant spear pointing into space. All along its length, Jack could see airships stopping at docks.

He had been up the Paris Metrotower during their first adventure with Mr Doyle, but the London tower was taller and wider—twenty miles across at the bottom, narrowing to a mile at the top. Located in Nortley, north of London, the iron and stone edifice was held together by Terrafirma, a type of mould invented by the Darwinists. Around its base, coal-powered stations dotted the landscape, spewing smoke and steam as they supplied energy to the building.

'It is quite large,' Mr Doyle agreed.

Passing through an arched entrance, they entered the domed foyer that contained a ten-foot high statue of Douglas Milverton, the inventor of Terrafirma, before purchasing tickets to go to the top.

Mr Doyle pointed to glowing, bell-shaped lamps over the elevators in the middle.

'Darwinists are testing a new energy source,' he explained. 'A kind of algae that converts light to power.'

'Amazing,' Scarlet breathed. 'What will they think of next?'

The elevator contained a score of seats. Some passengers produced newspapers while others closed their eyes to nap. A few elderly ladies pulled out knitting. Wheezing steam, the doors clanked shut, shuddered and the elevator started its ascent.

Jack knew the journey would take several hours, and they would have to change elevators several times because of the tower's curve. As Scarlet took out a well-thumbed book, Jack groaned silently.

'*The Adventure of the Sun Men*,' she said, reading the cover. 'One of the best books in the series.'

'The sun men?' Jack said.

'They live on the sun,' Scarlet explained.

'I'm sure they do,' Jack said, taking out his tatty

copy of *Ninety-Nine Ninjas*. 'Now this is what I call literature.'

'I'm not sure that's what I'd call it.'

'What do you mean?'

'Well, look at the cover.'

It showed dozens of black clad figures attacking a single person who was dressed entirely in white.

'Of course it's literature,' Jack said. 'It's *action* literature.'

Mr Doyle started reading a book about lion taming as he munched on a chunk of cheese. He carried cheese with him wherever he went. In fact, he rarely ate anything else.

They changed to another elevator at the one hundredth floor. This time there were no seats, so they stood. The next few hours seemed an endless repetition of changes. Jack wished they could have flown the *Lion's Mane* to the tower, but Mr Doyle did not want to leave the little airship moored for so long.

At the top, they exited the lift unsteadily. They had arrived at a village square, where the ceiling was painted blue with a sun in one corner. Steamcars and horse-driven vehicles trundled past. Jack found it hard to believe they were still inside a building.

They angled past traders to the windows, where Jack felt a rush of vertigo as he looked at the Earth below, the cornflower blue horizon at its edge and the endless inky sea of space above.

Incredible, he thought.

Rounding the building, they found their space steamer moored to one of the docks.

'The *Katsu*,' Jack read. He was a huge fan of the space-faring vessels. 'It's a Japanese ship and can carry up to eight hundred passengers.'

'It looks quite different to British steamers,' Scarlet said.

Jack nodded. British steamers looked more like battleships. The *Katsu*, despite being made from iron, and driven by steam, was designed more like an old wooden ship, curving up at both ends with three wide smokestacks, shaped like ancient sails rising from the flattened deck.

'I believe they've used a new form of Levaton on the hull,' Mr Doyle said, referring to the substance used to keep it afloat. 'They'll use that to send people to the moon.'

Jack tried to imagine men walking on the moon. 'It's hard to believe such a thing is possible,' he said.

'Not just possible,' Mr Doyle said. 'The plans are well underway. A section of this station is dedicated to building the craft they'll use for the journey.'

Hundreds of people were now streaming onto the ship, including diplomats accompanied by security guards and military personnel.

'There's the Australian representative,' Scarlet said, pointing to a man with a kangaroo embroidered on the back of his coat. Another had the Eiffel Tower emblazoned on his sleeve. 'And the French president.'

'The newspapers reported this as the most important meeting since the formation of the League of Nations,' Mr Doyle said. He pointed out several famous scientists to Jack and Scarlet. 'Some of the best minds in the world are here.'

Making their way onto the ship, they arrowed towards the main observation lounge at the bow. A whistle rang through the ship, and then it cast off, leaving the metrotower behind.

'The world looks quite different from up here,' Mr Doyle said.

'It's a beautiful place,' Scarlet agreed.

'And we want to keep it that way.'

Turning, they saw a stout, middle-aged man with a moustache and greying hair approaching.

'Albert!' Mr Doyle said.

'Ignatius!'

After the men had warmly clasped hands, Mr Doyle made the introductions. 'This is my old friend, Dr Albert Einstein,' he said. 'He's with the American branch of the Darwinist League.'

'Really?' Jack said. 'From your accent...'

'I fled Germany years ago,' Dr Einstein explained. 'Thanks to the Nazis, Jews are no longer welcome there.'

'I believe I've heard of you, sir,' Scarlet said. 'Your speciality is flying creatures?'

'It is. Airships are the thing of the past and must make way for new modes of travel.'

'Such as?' Scarlet said.

Einstein smiled. 'You will see them when we reach Japan. But I promise you this—airships will be a thing of the past.'

'No more airships?' Jack said. *What would they fly on?*

'We Darwinists have only just scratched the surface when it comes to Biomechanics,' Einstein continued. 'This is a brave new world, and it's being driven by cutting-edge science. The Japanese Darwinists are the leaders in these new technologies. Their inventions will change the world over the next few years.'

'I'm not familiar with the term *Biomechanics*,' Scarlet said.

'The Darwinists are on one side of the fence, promoting a cleaner, better world through the use of engineered life forms. On the other side are the Metalists, hell-bent on keeping the world run by coal power and machines. They have described our work as *ungodly* and *the work of the devil* and believe all biological research should be immediately halted.'

'That sounds very extreme,' Jack said.

'It is. Biological research has led to penicillin and other antibiotics that have saved millions of lives. And changes must be made now from steam to biology because of the Hot Earth crisis.'

'I thought that Hot Earth was just a theory.'

'The word "theory" has a different meaning to scientists. We define it as an explanation substantially tested and upon which one can make predictions.'

'That sounds more like a fact.'

'To all intents and purposes, it is unless a substantial piece of evidence disproves it. And that's rare in most cases,' Einstein said. 'Where Hot Earth theory is concerned, it's a fact. The earth is doomed unless we make changes and make them soon.'

'Doomed?' Jack exclaimed, his voice going up a note.

A few nearby passengers glanced up in alarm.

'Perhaps we should retire to our cabin,' Mr Doyle suggested, 'and continue our discussion there.'

Their room was located at the starboard section of the ship. They ordered food and were soon eating steak and kidney pies. As Mr Doyle poured tea, he asked Einstein to tell them more about the Hot Earth theory.

'Certainly,' the doctor said, smiling. 'As you know, the prime source of energy for modern civilisation is coal. We burn it to produce power, run our factories, steamcars—indeed, everything. A number of years ago, a Swedish scientist named Svante Arrhenius made a claim that carbon dioxide in our atmosphere could cause a blanket effect across the planet, resulting in a global warming effect.'

'Is that a bad thing?' Jack asked, thinking of how cold the winters were in England. 'I wouldn't mind a few more sunny days.'

'If only it were that simple. Warming the atmosphere, even by a few degrees, will have catastrophic effects across the globe: rising sea levels, droughts, famine, forest fires... Governments have, so far, ignored our warnings, but it is clear to most Darwinists that things must change.' Einstein sighed. 'We must change or we'll face certain disaster.'

Suddenly the space steamer shook, and tilted, sending Jack and the others crashing to the floor.

CHAPTER THREE

'Good heavens!' Mr Doyle cried.

He told Jack and Scarlet to remain in their cabin while he and Dr Einstein went to see what had happened. They returned several minutes later, looking grim.

'There was an explosion in the main engine room,' Mr Doyle said. 'One man was killed and another injured.'

'What a terrible accident!' Scarlet said.

'I doubt it is an accident,' Einstein said. 'It's probably the work of the Metalists. They would like nothing more than to destroy the Darwinist League and stop the ratification of the Hot Earth Accord. Some would not stop at murder.'

Mr Doyle looked troubled. 'This is not really what

I had in mind,' he said, 'when I agreed to be the guest of honour.'

'We need men of reason,' Einstein said. 'More now than ever. Only through science can we make the world a safer place.'

This is getting more dangerous by the minute, Jack thought. *It'll be a miracle if we reach Japan in one piece.*

But despite his pessimism, they reached the Tokyo Metrotower late the next day without further incident. Jack's mouth fell open when he saw the crimson square tower that resembled a pagoda. Its huge eaves jutted out for thousands of floors, all the way to the ground.

'The Japanese certainly have their own way of doing things,' Mr Doyle said. 'Traditionally, the wide eaves were used to keep water off the walls of their homes. Obviously that doesn't apply here, but they've retained the same style.'

Leaving the space steamer behind, Jack, Scarlet and Mr Doyle navigated to the middle of the metrotower. It was eerily reminiscent of its British counterpart, except the interior buildings were oriental in style: lots of square, bright-red buildings with small windows. Then Jack noticed the forms of transport people were using: carts drawn by ants the size of cows.

'I've never seen anything like it,' Scarlet said.

'I imagine there'll be much more to see,' Mr Doyle said. 'As Albert said, the Japanese are at the forefront of Darwinist innovation.'

Mr Doyle led them to an elevator marked Express

Sled. It was a cylindrical room, with leather restraints attached to the walls, allowing people to stand upright.

Mr Doyle spoke fluent Japanese, but he asked the attendant to explain in English so Jack and Scarlet could understand.

'We strap you in here,' the man said, pointing to the restraints. 'Then the elevator is released. The journey takes about fifteen minutes. About a mile from the ground, the brakes are applied and you gradually slide to a stop.'

'Really?' Scarlet said, dubiously. 'Is it safe?'

'Of course. Hundreds of people use the sled every day.'

'Life is an adventure,' Mr Doyle said, stepping inside. He paid their fare and the attendant locked them into place.

'Mr Doyle,' Scarlet said. 'I don't know if—'

'Have a happy journey,' the attendant said, closing the door.

Scarlet started again. 'Maybe we should—'

Then the elevator dropped and they fell at an incredible speed. A high-pitched whine came from outside: it sounded as though the elevator was skating along the edge of the shaft. Jack felt like his stomach was in his throat.

'This reminds me of a case I once investigated,' Mr Doyle yelled, 'involving a test dummy, a catapult and a broken net—'

'Some other time!' Scarlet shrieked, her face white.

'I'm sure we'll be fine!' Jack yelled. 'They use this sled all the time.'

'But what if something *does* go wrong?'

'Then it'll happen so fast we won't know anything about it.'

His heart was beating fast, but he wasn't scared. He'd faced far worse than this. There was little to look at, so he closed his eyes.

The compass and locket picture of his parents jangled in his pockets. For as long as he lived, Jack knew he would never forget the sight of them falling from the flying trapeze.

Falling...falling...

'We're almost there,' Mr Doyle said.

Jack opened his eyes. The sound of the elevator had changed to a lower pitch. Within seconds it eased to a crawl and stopped. The door opened and an attendant, not unlike the one at the top of the tower, smiled and came inside to unbuckle them.

'Did you enjoy the ride?' he asked.

'*Enjoy* probably isn't the word I'd use,' Scarlet said. 'Or the word *ride*, for that matter. More like *falling in extreme terror.*'

Stepping from the cabin, his legs shaking, Jack found himself in a huge hall filled with milling crowds. Men and women were in kimonos, a type of wraparound dress. The men wore plain, dark colours while the women were dressed in bright patterns of flowers, lilies or birds. Everyone wore sandals. A few children hurried along with their parents, with odd-looking dogs on leashes. Or were they cats?

'They're catogs,' Mr Doyle explained. 'A combination of cat and dog.'

One of the creatures, as big as an Alsatian, gave a *meow* as it passed.

An image of a Japanese warrior holding a curved sword covered the roof with a mural of rice fields and apple blossoms decorating the walls.

After collecting their bags from a luggage carousel, they inched through the crowds to the exit.

'You mentioned to the prime minister that you've been to Japan before?' Jack said to Mr Doyle.

'I have. A small incident involving a jewel necklace, a Japanese artist and an orange panda.' He popped a piece of cheese into his mouth. 'I really must pick up some of the local cheeses,' he added. 'They have a wonderful variety called *sakura*, a creamy cheese infused with cherry leaves.'

Jack looked about in wonder as he stepped out into night air choked by steam and smoke. It was raining softly; many people carried umbrellas. The crowded metropolis was jammed with either tall buildings or shanty houses. Skyscrapers were hundreds of storeys high, great iron monoliths with wide eaves, similar to the Tokyo Metrotower. Neon billboards were everywhere.

'That lighting...' Jack's voice trailed off.

'They're lit by a glow-worm developed here in

Japan,' Mr Doyle explained. 'They burn brighter, longer and better than any gaslight.'

Across the road was a huge fish market that carried every conceivable seafood: fish, whale meat, octopus, prawns, mussels, crabs and others Jack couldn't identify. Some people were buying raw products from counters in the middle while others ate cooked food at benches along the side.

At the front of a nearby building was a huge plate-glass window. Two large men, dressed only in loin clothes, were wrestling, pushing against each other as the audience yelled and clapped. Finally one shoved the other out of the ring and the patrons leapt to their feet in excited applause.

The smells were intoxicating, a mixture of spices, incense and machinery.

Tiny airships, emitting high-pitched whines, cut between the buildings. Jack had never seen them move so fast. Triple-decker steambuses chugged alongside people on steam-powered bicycles. Rickshaws, pulled by more giant ants, jostled with pedestrians along the footpaths. Mr Doyle raised his hand to hail one over.

They piled their gear into the back. Jack was surprised the ant was able to drag so much weight.

'Rickshaws are finely balanced,' Mr Doyle explained. 'Minimum effort provides maximum movement.'

The streets closed in around them. It continued to rain. They didn't have an umbrella, but Jack didn't mind in the least. The music from restaurants as they passed was discordant, a jangling of uneven notes, yet Jack found it strangely soothing. It reminded him of jazz.

They finally stopped outside of the *Hanako*, a large hotel in the Chuo district. It was ten storeys high with square, black-framed windows. Ceramic birds decorated the corners like gargoyles on a church. It was more modern than the surrounding buildings and security guards were posted at the front entrance. Mr Doyle showed them identification before bellhops hurried their bags inside.

Reception turned out to be a courtyard with a circular garden in the middle containing a cherry blossom tree, a large rock and raked sand. A restaurant was positioned to one side, with elevators opposite and the main desk straight ahead.

'You'd think they'd plant a few shrubs,' Jack said, peering at the garden.

'The Japanese use their gardens to represent ideas,' Mr Doyle said. 'The raking of the sand represents the harmony of the universe.'

Their rooms on the sixth floor turned out to be small and clean, sparsely furnished with windows overlooking the main street. There were no chairs around the low-slung coffee table, only thin cushions on which to sit.

Scarlet glanced into her bedroom and frowned. 'My bed appears to have been stolen,' she said, 'leaving me with only the mattress.'

'It's called a futon,' Mr Doyle explained. 'Everyone sleeps on them here.'

Sighing, she retired to her room, and Jack soon did the same.

Glancing out his window, he saw a thin ledge that ran around the building. A crow, sheltering from the rain, gave a mournful cry before flying back into the downpour and landing on the street below. Picking up a scrap of food, it flew off again, soaring over the crowded mesh of people, animals and machines.

Does this city ever sleep?

Jack read *Ninety-Nine Ninjas* for a few minutes before turning out his light and listening to the sounds of the foreign city. Thousands of miles from London, he may as well have been on another planet.

CHAPTER FOUR

'Ah,' Mr Doyle said. 'This place will do nicely.'

It was morning and they were standing outside a small eatery opposite the hotel. The street was busy with people hurrying to work, giant ants transporting carts of fresh produce, and steambuses trundling by.

It had stopped raining, though the sky was still overcast. Jack felt out of place in his green coat, but no-one seemed to give him a second glance.

'Japan is quite used to westerners,' Mr Doyle said, when Jack mentioned their appearance. 'It has rapidly become one of the most cosmopolitan countries in the world.'

He led them to a table on the footpath and handed

them menus, written in both Japanese and English.

Jack screwed up his face. 'Is this what I think it is?' he asked, pointing.

'Raw fish?' Mr Doyle said. 'Of course.'

'Can they cook it a little?' Jack asked.

'You'll love it,' Scarlet said. 'It's a Japanese delicacy.'

After ordering food, they sat and watched delegates arriving at the hotel. Most of them were scientists, but there were several diplomats too. It looked like people had travelled from all over the world.

'That man's wearing a dress,' Jack said, pointing to a dark-skinned man in a cream-coloured robe.

'It's called a *kanzu*,' Mr Doyle said. 'Traditionally worn in East Africa.'

Scarlet indicated two women wearing dresses decorated in red-and-orange flowers. 'And them?' she asked.

'Fiji, I imagine.' Mr Doyle pointed to a man who wore blue breeches and a yellow shirt. 'And Sweden. Their national colours were adopted around the turn of the century.'

Jack remembered what Dr Einstein had said about the Hot Earth Accord. If it wasn't signed now, the entire planet would suffer from environmental devastation. Every country would be affected.

We could end up living on a flooded planet, he thought. He tried to imagine what London would look like underwater. It was frightening.

Their food arrived. Mr Doyle and Scarlet looked

excited, but Jack stared gloomily at the table. He had a small bowl of plain rice, but the lump of fish was pink and unappealing.

'Uh,' Jack said. 'They haven't given us knives and forks.'

'They don't have them in Japan,' Scarlet said. 'They use chopsticks.'

Chopsticks looked like knitting needles. Mr Doyle was proficient and showed Jack and Scarlet how they worked. Scarlet took to them immediately, but Jack's first action was to poke himself in the eye.

'They take some getting used to,' Mr Doyle said.

Jack sighed. *I can't eat this*, he thought. *I need something to smother the taste.*

His eyes searched the condiments on the table, fixing on a small serve of avocado paste.

That will do, he thought. *I'll drown it in avocado.*

He smeared the paste all over the raw fish before spearing it on a chopstick.

I'll do it in one go, he thought. *Straight down the hatch!*

Jamming the chopstick into his mouth, Jack caught sight of the shocked expression on Scarlet's face.

'Jack!' she shrieked. 'What *are* you doing?'

He tried to answer, but the inside of his mouth had suddenly caught fire. His nasal cavities cleared as if sprayed with ammonia and he choked, the lump of fish jammed in his throat. It was like a volcano had erupted in his mouth. As his face turned bright red, he tried to spit out the fish. But it was stuck.

'Jack?' Mr Doyle said. 'Are you all right?'

'*No*,' he gasped. '*I'm...guk..gruch...*'

'Jack covered his fish with wasabi,' Scarlet said to Mr Doyle, 'and swallowed it!'

'Why?' Mr Doyle cried. 'Wasabi is blisteringly hot!'

Scarlet and Mr Doyle thudded his back until the lump of fish flew out like a cannonball. A waiter rushed over and poured water down Jack's throat.

Finally his face returned to its normal colour and he ate boiled rice to sooth his burnt mouth and throat.

Scarlet sadly shook her head. 'What made you do that?' she asked.

'I thought it was avocado!'

They finished their meals and returned to the hotel room where Mr Doyle ordered some juice from the kitchen. As Jack drank it down, he asked Mr Doyle about his brother.

'You've never mentioned him before,' Scarlet added.

Mr Doyle sighed. 'I apologise for my silence,' he said. 'I rarely think about Edgar, let alone speak of him. It has been many years since we last saw each other. What would you like to know?'

'You mentioned he is your step-brother?' Jack said.

'My father remarried after my mother's death. His new wife, Jane, already had a son from a previous marriage. That was Edgar.'

'You called him a scoundrel.'

'Indeed he was,' Mr Doyle sighed. 'He was always

wild, breaking rules and lying to our parents at every opportunity. As he grew older, he got even worse. It seemed the more my parents tried to discipline him, the more he grew determined to drive them to distraction.

'Then my parents had an idea. They noticed that both Edgar and I loved mysteries. A distant cousin of ours—a man by the name of Sherlock Holmes—was a detective. They approached him to see if he would take us on as his apprentices.'

'I've often wondered how you became a detective,' Jack said.

'It was a match made in heaven. Mr Holmes taught us everything he knew about the art of detection. How to disguise ourselves, find clues, tail criminals—everything that would prepare us for lives as detectives.'

'What happened to Mr Holmes?' Scarlet asked.

'He has long since retired,' Mr Doyle said. 'A dedicated bee keeper, he lives in Sussex.'

'And Edgar?' Jack asked.

Mr Doyle's face clouded over. 'Whereas I wanted to use our skills for the betterment of mankind, Edgar wanted to use them for the betterment of himself,' he said. 'Edgar left home at eighteen and we did not hear from him for years.'

'And then?' Scarlet prompted.

'Then we heard he had been arrested. He had become a jewel thief—a very successful one—but his luck had run out. My parents were both in ill health at that time. They went to visit him in jail, but he refused their help.'

Mr Doyle's eyes grew distant.

'I'm so sorry,' Jack said.

'I haven't seen him for years. I've barely even thought about him. Knowing how much pain he caused me and my parents...'

'Yes?'

'I dread him coming back into my life. If I hadn't been ordered by the prime minister, I wouldn't be here.'

There was a gentle knock at the door.

Mr Doyle called 'enter' and a slim young man, aged about seventeen, entered. He had short, black hair, fine features and wore a grey suit with an open collar. His hands were small and fine, and he looked like he had not yet begun to shave.

Bowing, he said, 'You are Doyle-*san*?'

'Yes, and you are...?'

'Hiro Tanaka,' he said. 'I was working with your brother.'

Mr Doyle made green tea as the young man sat down. He gave Jack and Scarlet a cautious smile.

'We were told you would make contact,' Mr Doyle said. 'May I ask why you were working with Edgar?'

'My parents are now dead, but they were very interested in history,' Hiro said. 'They raised me to take an interest in world events, and believed there would eventually be another war. You are British. I think it is better to have Britain as a friend than an enemy.'

'What do you know of the Kusanagi sword?'

'It is a legendary artefact.'

33

'So you don't believe in it?'

'On the contrary,' Hiro said. 'I believe in it very much. I pray it can be found and restored to the Japanese people. This was Edgar's hope. It is my hope also.'

Mr Doyle shifted in his seat. He had a bad leg from the war and it still troubled him. 'You know of Edgar's history?' he said.

'He told me he had once been a thief, but those days were long behind him.'

'Knowing Edgar's past,' Mr Doyle said, 'I find that unlikely. Still, we need to find him. When did you last see him?'

'We had followed up several leads,' Hiro said, taking a sip of his tea. 'But they came to nothing. Then, a few weeks ago, Edgar noticed we were being followed.'

'By whom? The Nazis?'

'I think so. We would sometimes catch sight of European men, wearing dark-grey trench suits, watching us from a distance. They never approached us and we did not speak to them.' Hiro stroked his chin. 'One day I came to pick up Edgar from his hotel, but found him gone. I have not seen him since.'

'Was there any sign of a struggle?'

'No. His clothing was still here, but his notebook was gone. He never went anywhere without it.'

'I see,' Mr Doyle said. 'Where are his belongings now?'

'Knowing you were staying at this hotel, I had them put into storage at the front desk.'

Mr Doyle went downstairs to have a look at his brother's belongings. While he was gone, Jack and Scarlet sat in an uncomfortable silence with the boy.

'Do you like living in Japan?' Jack asked, trying to break the ice.

'Very much. I have been nowhere else.'

'Your English is excellent,' Scarlet said.

'I learnt at school. My parents were most insistent that I learn.'

Mr Doyle returned, looking disappointed. 'It was just clothing and a few bottles of men's cologne.' Stroking his chin, he asked Hiro, 'Where were you going the day he went missing?'

'To the Takao shrine,' Hiro said. 'It is in the mountains, west of the city.'

'Then I suggest we make that our first point of call.'

Grabbing their coats, they left the room. Scarlet brought along an umbrella in case it started raining again. They followed Hiro, who said their transportation was on the roof.

Jack's mouth fell open when he saw it.

'What is *that?*' he asked.

'You are not familiar with *kagerou*? They are a dragonfly, one thousand times normal size.'

It *was* a dragonfly. The creature was twenty-feet long with a white snout like a dog, a black furry nose and two green, faceted eyes that took up most of its face. The body, long, thin and black-and-white, supported an egg-shaped brass cabin with a curved glass dome at the front.

The wings, as wide as its body was long, were transparent with an emerald and purple tinge. The creature made odd ticking sounds as it shuffled about on six spindly legs which were covered in thick hairs.

Jack realised the airships he had seen the previous night were actually these vessels. 'Are you sure it's safe?' he asked.

Hiro smiled. 'There is no need to be afraid,' he said, opening the passenger door. 'Our people use them every day.'

'I'm not afraid,' Jack bristled. 'Our airships in England are much larger.'

'And slower.'

Jack couldn't argue with him, remembering the speed of the dragonflies.

'Let's go,' Mr Doyle suggested. 'The sooner we get moving, the sooner we'll be there.'

Climbing aboard, Hiro sat at the controls while Jack and the others settled into two long, facing seats behind. Peering over Hiro's shoulder, Jack saw foot pedals attached to lines that stirred the huge insect into action or brought it to a halt. A steering wheel connected to a pulley system that attached to the wings.

Hiro pushed one of the pedals, turned the wheel and the giant dragonfly lifted off.

'My goodness!' Scarlet said, gripping Jack's arm.

The landscape flashed by. The curved design of the front windscreen deflected the wind, but it was still cold inside the cabin.

Soon they were soaring high over a foggy Tokyo. Jack's eyes were wide in amazement as he stared down. The tallest structures breaking through the fog included giant statues, many hundreds of feet high. Some were of huge cats, one paw raised in greeting; others were owls, men and other animals.

'Those are *Maneki-neko* statues,' Mr Doyle said, pointing to a cat. 'They are said to bring good luck.' He pointed to a squat figure of a man with a Mohawk. 'As do the *Fukusukue* statues.'

'And those?' Jack asked, pointing at three giant owls to the west of the city.

'They represent wisdom,' Hiro spoke up. 'We Japanese believe very much in symbolism.'

Highways, jammed with fast-moving traffic, wound about the city like huge snakes, many of them passing straight through buildings.

In the distant south, Jack could just make out a few islands.

'Those are the Izu and Ogasawara Islands,' Hiro explained.

'I don't see any rice fields,' Scarlet said, peering down. 'I thought they'd be everywhere.'

'Most of the rice comes from northern Japan,' Hiro said. 'In Hokkaido and Niigata.'

'We don't have as many tall buildings in London,' Mr Doyle said. 'Is all of Japan like this?'

'Mostly. Many are apartments,' Hiro said. 'But some are privately owned.'

'The owners must be very wealthy.'

'Some have earned their money honestly, but others are crime bosses.'

'Is there a lot of crime in Japan?' Jack asked.

'Too much. Some of the bosses are very powerful.'

Soon they had left the metropolis behind and were heading towards a line of steep mountains. A few of the valleys were dammed, and Hiro explained how they supplied much of the drinking water for Tokyo.

He eventually brought the dragonfly into a shallow descent, over hills covered in cypress and cedar, and steered towards a winding road.

Indicating some buildings nestled among a stand of trees, he said, 'That's it,' he said. 'That's Takao shrine.'

'I thought it would be like a church,' Jack said.

'It is where *kami*—spirits or universal elements—are said to live. This shrine is dedicated to the mountain, Takao.'

The dragonfly landed smoothly on the road and Hiro tied it to a pole. Jack was surprised the creature was so placid. After placing a hood over its bulbous head, Hiro hung a feedbag under its mouth.

'It won't fly away?' Scarlet said.

'The dragonfly are well trained,' Hiro said.

The forest was quiet except for the sound of distant birdsong. At the edge of the road, Jack and the others came to a timber gate made from two upright poles, with another two placed across the top.

'That is the *torii*,' Hiro explained. 'It symbolises the

transition from the normal world to the sacred.'

'It's a bit lopsided,' Scarlet said.

'There was an earthquake here recently, so the shrine was evacuated. I doubt anyone will be here today.'

They followed a path to a wide, flat building with a curving pitched roof.

'The *haiden*,' Hiro said, pointing. 'Used for worship.'

Inside, the building had been decorated with hand-carved timber poles and bright-red ceiling battens. Bamboo mats covered the floor. Signs written in Japanese hung from the ceiling. It smelt strongly of musk-scented incense.

They continued on to a smaller building flanked by statues of hybrid lion-dogs at the entrance.

'And this is the *honden*,' Hiro said. 'The heart of the shrine.' The front door was slightly ajar. 'Normally this is closed to the public, but the *kami* has probably been removed.'

Here, they found a less ornate building with an altar at the other end. Paving stones covered the floor.

'The *kami* is usually a mirror, or a statue, but neither is here.'

'And this is where Edgar had planned to visit?' Mr Doyle said.

'Edgar was very excited about coming here,' Hiro said, peering about. His face filled with dismay. 'He seemed to think it would lead to the sword, but everything appears completely normal. I don't see that this can possibly lead to the Kusanagi sword—or to Edgar!'

CHAPTER FIVE

'We are only at the beginning of our investigation,' Mr Doyle said. 'These things take time. We will begin by making a thorough investigation of this room.'

They started by examining the walls. Then Jack, Scarlet and Mr Doyle each took out their magnifying goggles and stared at the ceiling for several minutes. Finally, peering at the stones in the floor, they ran their fingers along the grooves.

Mr Doyle stopped near the altar.

'This is interesting,' he said. 'This tile is slightly askew.'

'Maybe the earthquake caused it,' Jack suggested.

'Possibly, but it seems strange that none of the other

tiles are affected.' He gripped the edge. 'Help me move it.'

Jack and the others grabbed the tile and pulled upwards to reveal an ancient timber ladder leading to a tunnel beneath.

'I assume *hondens* don't usually have underground tunnels,' Mr Doyle said.

'They do not,' Hiro said.

Mr Doyle led them down to another tunnel made of stone. Breathing in the cold, dry air, Jack smelt incense, but it was very faint.

As Mr Doyle lit a candle, Scarlet tilted her head. 'Did you hear that?' she asked.

'What?' Jack said.

'I'm not sure. It sounded like voices.'

They listened hard but there was nothing.

'It may have been my imagination,' she said at last.

The tunnel eventually opened onto a square chamber. A mural of an ancient sword covered the far wall. On an altar below was an ancient parchment.

'I believe this is our first clue,' Mr Doyle said.

The image on the parchment was a map of a bay, surrounded by trees and something that looked like the entrance to a cave. In the middle of the bay was a mountain with a red top. A string of flowers bordered the picture. The other side was blank.

'It appears to be some kind of map, but—'

'There!' Scarlet said, swinging about. 'I heard it again.'

Hiro hurried to the doorway. 'We are being followed!'

he cried as a shot rang out, and a bullet ricocheted off a wall. 'There's a group of men back there! Europeans!'

'It must be those damn Nazis!' Mr Doyle said, pulling out his gun, Clarabelle. He said to Hiro, 'Do you have any experience handling a firearm?'

'A little.'

Mr Doyle handed him the weapon. 'Shoot sporadically. We'll need time to find an exit.'

Hiro tentatively fired off a shot as Mr Doyle rolled up the parchment and pocketed it. He began to examine the walls.

'Are you sure there *is* an exit?' Jack asked.

'Without a doubt,' he said, pointing to the floor. 'You see this scrape here? It's where the wall has swung back.'

They tried pushing on various places on the wall, but nothing happened. Hiro continued to fire at their attackers. Suddenly Scarlet pointed to a brass torch holder set into the stone then indicated the floor beneath it.

'This surface is clean,' she said.

'What?' Mr Doyle said. After his gaze had followed hers, he grinned. 'Scarlet, you're a genius. Any torch would leave some waxy residue.'

He gave it a twist, and the wall swung forward. 'Come on!'

After piling through the opening, they pulled the door shut and raced up another tunnel, the clatter of footsteps close behind. At the very end came a faint sliver of light.

Mr Doyle pulled at another torch holder, and

the wall swung open, revealing trees and thick shrub. Scrambling through, they found themselves at the base of a narrow ravine.

'Up there!' Mr Doyle cried.

Racing up the hill, they reached the road. Scarlet pointed.

'There's our ride!' she yelled.

Within seconds, they were back in the egg-shaped cabin of the dragonfly, and Hiro was spurring the giant insect into the air.

'Do you think—' Jack started.

A shot rang out. A second dragonfly had taken off from behind the temple, with men crowded into its cabin.

'They're chasing us!'

Mr Doyle leant out and fired. 'I hit it,' he said, 'but it hasn't had any effect.'

'Dragonflies are very tough,' Hiro said.

Breaking through some low-lying clouds, they headed towards the city. Jack glanced through the rear window. 'I can't see anything,' he said. 'Maybe we've lost them.'

'I doubt it,' Scarlet said. 'We've got that parchment and they want it.'

Crash!

The other vessel came out of nowhere and slammed into them sideways. More shots rang out, shattering the front window.

Mr Doyle fired off another shot, but missed as the other dragonfly rapidly climbed. Then two men leapt through the air. The moustached of the pair landed on their dragonfly's neck while the bald man somehow made it into their cabin, his gun raised.

'Give me the parchment!' he said in a thick German accent. He was short, swarthy and built like a boxer. 'You will—'

Scarlet knocked the gun aside as Mr Doyle slammed a fist into his stomach. Through the window, Jack glimpsed the Nazi on the dragonfly's neck trying to force the creature towards the ground.

Hiro yelled, 'Hold on!'

Jack and the others gripped the underneath of the seats as Hiro jerked the wheel to one side, which sent the Nazi into the wall. Then they were upside down.

The Nazi struggled to regain his footing, but Mr Doyle kicked at him, and the man screamed as he went crashing through the side door and dropped from the sky. Outside, the second man lost his grip on the dragonfly's neck and fell away.

'Watch out!' Scarlet cried.

They were in a steep dive with a forest only seconds away. Hiro jerked the wheel back and they narrowly avoided the tops of trees.

'Where are they?' Jack said. 'Are they still—'

The Nazi's dragonfly slammed into them again. This time its wings tangled with theirs. A Nazi took the opportunity to dash around to their vessel. As Mr Doyle took aim with Clarabelle, the German managed to fire off the first shot, and the weapon flew from the detective's hand.

Jack scrambled from his seat.

'Jack!' Mr Doyle yelled. 'Don't—'

But he was already halfway across the wing. The Nazi fired another shot and missed. Jack managed to knock his gun away, then dropped and swung out his leg, knocking the other man down. Snarling, the German grabbed Jack's foot and tried to push him off the wing, but Jack smashed him across the face.

Scarlet raced across the wing, and pushed Jack down. Umbrella in hand, she hooked the handle onto the back of the Nazi's shirt and pressed the release button. The umbrella flew open, caught the wind and dragged the man into the ether.

'Get back in here!' Mr Doyle yelled.

Hiro waited until they were back inside—then slammed on the brakes. The other creature continued forward, one of its wings damaged, towards a bank of trees. It seemed the Nazis were doomed, but the pilot regained control at the last moment, bringing in the dragonfly to an ungainly landing.

As they flew away, Jack spotted the remaining men stagger from the aircraft.

'We survived,' Jack said, falling back in his seat.

'And we have the parchment,' Scarlet said.

'Only one question remains,' Mr Doyle said, pulling it from his pocket. 'What does it mean?'

CHAPTER SIX

It was evening by the time they arrived back at the hotel. Mr Doyle insisted they eat a meal. They would tackle the parchment in the morning.

'You know what I always say,' he said, ordering food at the restaurant. 'Brains work better when they're well fed.'

'I agree,' Jack said. 'Just as long as there's no wasabi.'

Mr Doyle smiled. The meal arrived, a dish called tempura—fish and vegetables dipped in batter and fried. All the while, strange music was piped through the intercom system. The restaurant was busy, with many of the Darwinist hotel delegates also eating. 'There's a lot of security here,' Scarlet said, nodding towards the broad-shouldered men standing near the door.

'Most of the leading Darwinists are present,' Mr Doyle said. 'Losing them would put science back by decades.'

Dr Einstein noticed them and strolled over. They introduced Hiro as their guide.

'Are you enjoying Japan?' Dr Einstein asked them.

Jack almost choked on his meal, remembering the day they'd had, but Scarlet managed a sweet smile. 'It's a beautiful country,' she said. 'Hiro very kindly took us for a tour on a *kagerou*.'

'They're an amazing beast,' Einstein said. 'A credit to the Japanese branch of the Darwinist League. And I hope you'll be attending the seminars? I'm sure you'll find them interesting.'

'What will they be speaking about?' Jack asked.

'All the most recent breakthroughs in Darwinist technology. One of the highlights is an innovative new kind of scuba diving equipment. You're familiar with jellyfish? Well, we've developed a new kind that we're calling the jellysuit. The diver inhales a breathing tube and the suit wraps around them, protecting them from the sea.'

'Oh. Where does the tube go?'

'Into the diver's lungs,' Dr Einstein said.

Scarlet blanched.

Einstein turned to Mr Doyle. 'Ignatius, we've scheduled your address for the closing ceremony,' he said. 'Right after your presentation, we're hoping the Hot

Earth Accord will be signed.'

'Are you sure that all the dignitaries will sign it?' Mr Doyle asked.

'We still have a lot of convincing to do, but we're hoping to have won them over by then.'

After Einstein had left, Scarlet explained the Hot Earth theory to Hiro.

'This makes sense,' Hiro said, thoughtfully. 'Elderly people talk about how much snow there used to be on Mount Fuji. Now there is hardly any at all.'

Mr Doyle offered to have a bed made up for Hiro, but he declined. 'I look after my aunt,' he said. 'Her health is not good, so I do chores for her.'

'Thank you for what you've done so far.'

Bowing his head, Hiro headed off.

The next morning, Jack, Scarlet and Mr Doyle ate breakfast in their room.

'There's one thing that's disappointed me about Japan,' Jack said. 'Apart from the Nazis.'

'What would that be?' Mr Doyle asked, topping his *okonomiyaki*, a Japanese pancake, with fluffy cheese from his pocket.

'We haven't come across any ninja yet.'

'Hmm,' Mr Doyle said. 'I don't believe there are any ninja in modern-day Japan.'

'That's what the ninja want us to believe. Secrecy is their best tool. We could use a few ninja on our side,' he said. 'Not to mention their weapons.'

'What sort of weapons?' Scarlet asked.

'*Shuriken*, for one.'

'*Shuriken*? They sound like a type of fried fish!'

'No! They're throwing stars—flat, pointed disks that ninja throw at their enemies. And they also use *sai*, a kind of small trident, for stabbing.'

'Sounds ghastly.'

'Only if you're on the receiving end.'

Mr Doyle glanced at his watch. 'There are a number of talks beginning in a few minutes,' he said. 'I suggest we head down. We should keep up a pretence of being here for the symposium, just in case our enemies are watching.'

They followed Mr Doyle downstairs, where they bumped into Hiro. He and Scarlet headed off to a talk about the Hot Earth crisis, while Jack and Mr Doyle chose one about Darwinist inventions for the oceans.

'I would have thought that Scarlet had heard enough about this Hot Earth thing,' Jack said, frowning, as they disappeared through a doorway.

Mr Doyle shrugged. 'Maybe she wanted to get to know Hiro better,' he said. 'Ah, here's our room. Looks like it's a packed house.'

Get to know Hiro better? Jack thought. *In what way?*

Finding a pair of seats a few rows from the front, Jack realised his stomach was rumbling uncomfortably.

Why would Scarlet want to know Hiro better?

A horrible thought occurred to him. Surely she wasn't *interested* in him?

49

Dr Einstein took to the stage.

'Allow me to welcome you here today to one of the more interesting seminars at this year's symposium,' he said. 'Travelling the oceans will be a truly new experience once these creations are revealed to the world. Please welcome our next speaker, Dr Anna Livanov.'

A handsome middle-aged woman, with grey hair, came out on the stage. She held her head up high, but Jack noticed her clothing was old and worn.

'Thank you, Dr Einstein,' she said with a Russian accent. She wore dark eye makeup and crimson lipstick. When her eyes settled on Jack, she smiled. 'It is a great pleasure to see a young person here today. The future lies with the young.'

Several heads turned to look at Jack and he felt himself blushing.

'The world is changing,' Livanov continued. 'We all know of the growing Hot Earth crisis. If it is not averted, large parts of our world will soon be underwater, destroying cities, valuable farmland and displacing millions of people.

'But my talk today is not about Hot Earth.' She flashed another smile. 'You're in the wrong room if you thought that's why we're here.' The crowd laughed. 'I want to speak about whaling ships. But not ships that pursue whales, but ships that *are* whales.'

She pulled back a curtain, exposing a cross-section sketch of a whale. Jack stared at it in fascination. Most of the creature was empty with the front made of a transparent skin.

'Our new generation of whaling ships is based on the blue whale,' said Dr Livanov, 'the largest creature to currently exist, and the heaviest that has *ever* existed on Earth. Our modifications have made the creature three times its normal size. They have been bred without brains and mouths, but with their nervous systems intact.'

She indicated a hole at the top.

'The creature is fed krill through here, providing sustenance for the whale. The bridge is at the front, the living quarters at the rear. The whale is capable of carrying up to two hundred people. Not only can it travel on the surface, but it can dive to any part of the ocean bottom.'

She tapped the picture.

'With this invention, the wonders of the seven seas, even the Mariana Trench—the deepest part of the ocean— will finally be revealed to us. My fellow scientists, this is truly a new world in which we live.'

There was a moment of silence, and then the assembled scientists broke into thunderous applause. Jack was with them. *A whale that can carry passengers and take them to the bottom of the ocean?* It was incredible!

Mr Doyle and Jack went up to congratulate Dr Livanov after her presentation.

'Ah,' she said, 'the young scientist.'

'I'm not a scientist,' Jack said, blushing. 'My maths isn't good enough.'

Einstein stuck his head over Jack's shoulder. 'Never fear, young man,' he said. 'I've had problems with numbers too. There's just too many of them!'

They all laughed.

'Whatever you decide to do,' Dr Livanov said, 'make certain you give it one hundred per cent. Science has not made me rich, but it has made me satisfied.'

'Thank you,' Jack said. It was wonderful advice. 'I'll do that.'

Saying goodbye, they returned to the lobby. Jack wished Scarlet could have been there to meet the doctor. She really was an inspiration.

His eyes searched the packed room, finally landing on Scarlet and Hiro as they were leaving their seminar. Hiro had his hand on Scarlet's arm.

Jack pushed through the crowd. 'There you are!' he said. 'I was wondering where you'd gotten to.'

'What do you mean?' Scarlet said. 'We went to the Hot Earth talk.'

'I know.' He turned to Hiro, who was looking at him with an amused expression. 'I didn't know you had an interest in science.'

'I have interests in many things.'

Jack found himself wanting to punch the boy in the face.

'Are you all right?' Scarlet asked. 'You've gone red.'

There were two more afternoon sessions. This time Jack went to the same session as Hiro and Scarlet, a talk entitled 'Enlarging Flying Insects for Mass Transportation'.

Many of the diplomats had come along—some were arguing furiously about the Hot Earth theory.

'But surely there have always been fluctuation in world temperatures,' one said.

'Never in such a short period of time,' the other replied.

'How will you vote?'

Jack did not hear his reply as the session started.

It looks like there's a lot of disagreement over Hot Earth, he thought. *I just hope everyone makes the right decision.*

By the time the seminar had finished, it was almost dinnertime.

Mr Doyle joined them. 'Hello everyone,' he said cheerily, popping a piece of mouldy cheese into his mouth. 'What would everyone like to do now?'

'We could go out for food?' Hiro suggested.

'What a wonderful idea,' Mr Doyle said.

'Shouldn't we be trying to work out the meaning of the parchment?' Jack asked. Hanging around the symposium and listening to lectures wasn't really moving them ahead in the search for the Kusanagi sword.

Mr Doyle tapped the side of his head. 'Something will occur to us,' he said. 'The subconscious is a powerful tool.'

Jack, Scarlet and Mr Doyle went upstairs to change, while Hiro went in search of a suit for dinner. Putting on a new white shirt, blue pants and a black jacket, Jack thought it looked quite good.

Scarlet appeared at their doorway, dressed in a pale-green evening dress.

'You look very nice,' he said.

'Thank you.'

Hiro turned up in a black suit. Even Jack thought he looked dashing.

'You look delightful,' Hiro said to Scarlet, bowing. 'As beautiful as a lotus.'

'Thank you,' Scarlet said, tittering.

Jack fumed. *As beautiful as a lotus! What a line!* He held his tongue as they made their way downstairs.

'I know of a restaurant we can go to,' Hiro said. 'It's not far from here.'

A steamcab pulled up outside and they piled into the back. Glass separated them from the driver. Hiro told him the address and they started off. It had started raining again, and Jack stared out gloomily at the falling rain as the others chatted.

Hiro let out a small cry, glancing outside. 'This is wrong,' he said. 'This isn't the way to the restaurant.'

He banged on the glass, but the driver ignored him.

Mr Doyle sighed. 'It looks like we're missing dinner,' he said. 'It appears we're being kidnapped.'

CHAPTER SEVEN

The rain poured down as the steamcab trundled through the crowded Tokyo streets.

Mr Doyle tried the door and found it opened easily. 'I doubt our kidnapper means us harm,' he said, pulling it shut. 'Not yet, anyway.' He leant forward and said through the glass, 'Can you tell us where we're going?'

'To a meeting,' the driver said over his shoulder.

'With whom?'

'You will see.'

Sighing, Mr Doyle sat back. 'I thought he might say that,' he murmured.

Jack's heart was in his throat, but they didn't seem to be in any immediate danger. The rain eased, leaving some of the roads flooded, and the steamcab had to pull onto the footpath to avoid puddles.

Finally, they left the crowds and lights of the shopping district behind, entering a district of older buildings, with dark stone walls, and tiled awnings and roofs. Two metal gates swung shut as they pulled into a gloomy lane. Jack realised they were trapped.

'Mr Doyle—' he started.

'We'll be all right. Just keep your wits about you.'

Jack, Scarlet and Mr Doyle climbed out. Hiro went to follow, but the driver stopped him.

'Not you,' he said.

'But—'

'You are in no danger,' the driver said.

Jack swallowed. *What about us?*

Closing the door on Hiro, the driver led them to a gate at the end of the alley where they went through to a garden.

Jack was ready to defend himself, but there didn't seem to be anyone to fight. The garden looked very peaceful. Ahead lay a tiny bridge that crossed a pond. On the other side, they found themselves on a narrow path bordered by raked sand.

In the corner of the garden was an old-looking cherry blossom in full bloom. At the far edge of the garden was a high hedge backing onto the neighbouring buildings.

Behind the cherry blossom a faint light appeared as someone holding a lantern came walking towards them. Jack soon saw it was an old man dressed in a white kimono, loose pants and a half-coat.

'Welcome to my garden,' he said. 'I am Hikaru Satou.' He raised the lantern. 'And you are Mr Ignatius Doyle, Scarlet Bell and Jack Mason.'

'Why have you brought us here?' Mr Doyle asked.

'You westerners are always the same,' Satou said, smiling slightly. 'Always straight to the point.' He indicated to a small building to one side. 'Will you join me for tea?'

'We *were* going to dinner,' Scarlet said, pointedly.

Satou smiled. 'You will have tea,' he said. 'Please wait one minute before following.'

He entered through a small door into the building.

'We should leave,' Jack said. His stomach growled. 'Even my stomach agrees.'

Mr Doyle shook his head. 'This man may have some information pertaining to our investigation. And besides,' he added, 'the Japanese tea ceremony is a custom not to be missed. Follow my lead.'

They crossed the small lawn and were forced to bow by the low doorway as they entered the tea house. Taking their seats opposite the old man, they watched as he cleaned the implements, scooped a green mixture into a bowl and added hot water. Once Satou had presented the bowl to Mr Doyle, they exchanged bows. The detective took the bowl, rotated it and took a sip. He wiped the edge, then handed it to Scarlet and Jack, who did the same.

Nothing like English tea, Jack noticed. *It's more soothing.*

After the tea was drunk, Satou cleaned the utensils again and presented them for inspection. Mr Doyle nodded and Satou took them away.

'What was all that about?' Jack whispered.

'It's a ritual,' Mr Doyle explained in a low voice, 'dating back thousands of years.'

Satou returned. 'I note the impatience of Jack,' he said. 'The young are often impatient.'

'Not just the young,' Mr Doyle said, smiling. 'Old men such as myself don't have as long to live. We grow impatient too.'

Satou laughed. 'You have come in search of the Kusanagi sword,' he said. 'Why?'

'We wish to return it to the Japanese people.'

'To gain favour with us.'

'That is true,' Mr Doyle hesitated. 'But also to find my brother.'

Satou nodded. 'Family is very important,' he said. 'But you know of the sword's power?'

'I know it has legendary properties.'

'They are more than legend,' Satou said. 'Yamato Takeru used the sword to save himself from an evil war lord, turning a fire away that would have surely killed him.'

'That is the legend.'

'The Kusanagi sword can control the wind. It can probably do much more.'

'We respect your beliefs,' Mr Doyle said, gently. 'But we do not share them.'

The old man looked through the window into the ancient garden. 'It is a shame,' he said. 'A frog in a well does not know the sea.'

'I can only know what is evidenced by my senses.'

'Does the wind not blow when we sleep?' Satou asked. 'Does a tree in the forest not die when no-one's eyes glimpse its passing?' He slowly stood and led them to a small enclosure where a twisted tree grew in a pot. 'This bonsai is over eight hundred years old. Tended by generations of people, long dead, long forgotten, their names have been consigned to the dust of history. Yet the tree exists. But even it is not eternal. Its life will ebb one day and return to the river that flows through us all.' Lowering the lantern, he turned to Mr Doyle. 'You have solved many mysteries, but some things cannot be solved.'

'What are you saying?'

'There is a gap between knowing and science,' he said.

'That's very poetic.'

'The path will find you,' Satou said enigmatically. The old man's eyes settled on Jack. 'The Kusanagi sword can only be wielded by one who is true of heart and believes in its power.'

The old man walked them to the front entrance. The door swung open, as if by magic, and he pointed to the alley.

'Thank you for the tea,' Mr Doyle said.

Plucking a flower from a plant, Satou handed it to

Scarlet. She tucked it thoughtfully into a pocket as they went through the doorway. Glancing back, Jack saw the old man had already disappeared.

'What happened?' Hiro asked, when they returned to the steamcab.

They explained everything that Satou had told them.

'It does not sound like he was threatening you,' Hiro said.

'He wasn't,' Mr Doyle said. 'I believe he was trying to help us, but I'm not sure his advice gets us anywhere.'

The steamcab took them back to the hotel. Jack's stomach was growling more than ever, so they went to the hotel restaurant and ate a meal of rice and steamed vegetables.

'I had no idea vegetables could taste so good,' he said, patting his stomach happily.

'Everything tastes good when you're hungry,' Mr Doyle replied.

'Have you had any thoughts about the parchment?' Scarlet asked.

'Not yet. Although it does remind me of a case I once investigated involving a purple frog, a mushroom and an opera singer—'

Scarlet feigned a yawn. 'I'm feeling rather tired,' she said.

'Oh, I see. Then it's probably best if we retire for the night.'

They asked Hiro if they could find him a room, but he again declined.

'My aunt will worry if I do not return.'

After they'd said goodnight to Hiro, Jack led Scarlet and Mr Doyle back to their room.

'Hiro is so lovely,' Scarlet said. 'He takes such an interest in his aunt.'

Jack groaned.

'What is going on with you?' Scarlet asked.

'Nothing,' he replied, grumpily.

Is Scarlet keen on Hiro? he wondered. *And how does he feel about her?*

Opening the door to their room, Mr Doyle let out a cry.

CHAPTER EIGHT

The apartment had been ransacked. Every piece of furniture had been overturned, clothing pulled from drawers and paintings torn off walls, as if a tornado had whipped through the room.

A sound came from Jack's bedroom. Then a thickset man wearing a dark-grey trench coat appeared. He barrelled towards them, pushing Jack and Scarlet out of the way before knocking Mr Doyle over. The parchment fell from the detective's jacket.

The intruder scooped it up.

'*Ich habe es*!' he cried, racing through the open door.

'He's a Nazi!' Mr Doyle yelled. 'And he's got the map!'

Jack gave chase as the thief raced down the corridor, pushing through the fire doors and charging upstairs.

Where's he going?

The man burst from the stairwell onto the roof with Jack close behind. A fog had set in, drowning everything in a fine mist.

The thief raced across the roof and leapt onto the adjacent building. Jack followed, picking up speed. The Nazi was bigger, but slower, and when jumping onto the next curving roof of a temple, he slid backwards. Jack made a grab for him, but the man swung around and threw a punch into his face.

Jack saw stars. He hit the roof and started to slide down. Shaking his head, he raked the tiles with outstretched fingers, got a grip and scrambled up. The Nazi pulled out a gun, but Jack knocked it away and delivered a blow to the man's stomach. The map went flying and clattered on the sloping tiles of the next roof.

It's going over the side!

Jack threw himself after it.

Snatching it in mid-air, Jack continued over the roof's edge.

Crash!

He'd landed in a seat on the open-top of a triple-decker bus. Jack rolled and raced down the aisle, stowing the parchment into his coat. The passengers recoiled in terror. The bus picked up speed as it headed towards a major road.

Glancing back, Jack saw the Nazi had landed in

the back row and was already after him.

As the bus pulled onto a freeway, another triple-decker drew near. Jack stepped onto the headrest of the nearest seat and jumped across to the next bus, sprawling into one of the seats. A family of tourists yelled at him.

'Sorry!' Jack cried. He glanced back to see the thief was still in pursuit.

Does this guy ever give up?

As they passed a row of tenement buildings, Jack took another running leap and landed on the nearest roof, with the Nazi close behind.

Now there was nowhere to go: only a fifty-foot drop.

Jack ducked and leapt sideways as the Nazi lunged—and continued over the side, screaming as he fell headfirst to the ground below.

Jack managed to regain his breath—until he slipped and fell facefirst onto the tiles. The top of the roof was only a few feet above, but it may as well have been miles. He was about to fall!

Then an arm reached out and grabbed his hand.

Jack looked up in amazement.

A ninja!

Gripping Jack's hand tightly, he pulled him to safety.

'Thank you,' Jack stammered. 'You saved my life.'

With the chance to examine the ninja more closely, Jack realised he was a *she*. The ninja stared back from under a hooded cowl that left only her piercing blue eyes visible. She wore a dark-red outfit—a jacket with overlapping lapels and loose fitting pants—and laced-up boots. From her belt hung a pouch, a sword and a grappling hook.

The red ninja gave Jack a brief nod. Then she looked past him and pointed. Jack turned to gaze at the endless horizon of roofs. *There's nothing to see.* When he turned back, she was gone.

Deep in thought, Jack made his way down to the street. It took another two hours to find the hotel where he found security guards and police everywhere. Two figures broke from the crowd.

'Jack!' Scarlet cried.

'My boy!' Mr Doyle yelled.

They threw their arms around him.

'You shouldn't have gone after him!' Mr Doyle scolded.

'At least it was worthwhile,' Jack said, allowing the detective a glimpse of the parchment in his jacket.

Returning to their room, the police demanded a full explanation of what had happened. Without going into detail, Mr Doyle had already told them the thief had stolen one of their belongings. Jack explained what had happened to the assailant, leaving out any mention of the ninja.

After they left, Scarlet suggested they move to another room, but Mr Doyle shook his head.

'The Nazis now know we're carrying the map with us at all times,' he said. 'I doubt they'll try again. They were watching Edgar and now they're watching us.'

He turned his attention to their room, insisting they

tidy up immediately.

'We'll feel all the better for it in the morning.'

Jack groaned. It was bad enough chasing a thief across half of Tokyo without having to clean too! But they went to work and, within the hour, had the place liveable again.

'Oh!' Jack yelled. 'I haven't told you about the ninja!'

'What?' Mr Doyle and Scarlet barked.

He recounted what happened up on the roof, expecting them to disbelieve him. But Mr Doyle only nodded thoughtfully.

'If you say that's what happened,' he said, 'then that's what happened.'

'But ninja are just the stuff of legend,' Scarlet said.

'It seems the legend lives.'

'And it's a female ninja,' Jack said. There were no female ninja, not even in his book, *Ninety-Nine Ninja*. 'And she's on our side.'

Scarlet peered at him. 'You're sure you didn't hit your head?'

'Of course not! Well, I did, but she was real!'

'And obviously a friend,' Mr Doyle said. 'She came to your aid when you needed it.'

Finally climbing into bed, Jack thought he would be asleep in a minute, but he couldn't stop thinking about the events of the day.

I've seen a real ninja, he thought. *And if there's one, there must be more.*

When he next opened his eyes, he found Mr Doyle

knocking at his door, looking bright-eyed and ready for action.

'Another day!' Mr Doyle announced. 'We have a mystery to solve!'

'Do I have to?' Jack asked. He felt like he'd been run over by a triple-decker bus.

'Attending more symposiums will stimulate our brain cells,' he said. 'Eventually we will understand the mystery of the map.'

Jack wearily showered and dressed, and within minutes was eating breakfast with Scarlet. The map was on the table between them. Mr Doyle, as usual, had opted for cheese. The hotel clerk had tracked down several rare varieties, and Mr Doyle was systematically sampling each.

Jack frowned at one covered in mould. *Shouldn't that be thrown away?*

'You'd enjoy this one, Jack,' Mr Doyle said, trying to stifle a grin. 'It's wasabi-flavoured.'

'Oh joy.'

'Have you had any thoughts about the map?' Scarlet asked Mr Doyle.

'Only that it is was produced by a talented artist,' he said. 'I received a message from Hiro this morning. He has been delayed. He still needs to help his aunt.'

Jack felt a surge of satisfaction.

Good.

Scarlet frowned at him. 'What are you smiling at?' she demanded.

'Nothing.'

'So you're grinning like a mad person for no reason at all?'

'I'm just happy!'

'Well stop it!'

They finished breakfast and went downstairs. A noticeboard displayed the day's talks: one scientist was speaking about using the Australian wombat as a form of transport, another about experimental space steamers made from plants. The latter was such a strange idea that they all decided to go.

Unfortunately, the speaker—Dr Hodder—turned out to not be the most exciting of speakers. And it seemed it would take him hours to get to the point.

'I must begin with how life started on Earth,' Hodder said. 'Some four billion years ago...'

Jack wondered if it was too late to switch to the other lecture. Shifting about restlessly, he was staring up at the ceiling when he heard the audience gasp. He looked back to see Hodder staggering away from the lectern, white and shaking. When he collapsed at the edge of the stage, people leapt to his aid.

After a few minutes, Dr Einstein approached Jack and the others, his face pale.

'Is Dr Hodder all right?' Jack asked.

'I'm afraid not,' Einstein said. 'He's dead.'

CHAPTER NINE

'And here,' Mr Doyle said, pointing, 'the way the artist juxtaposes small complex areas of pattern against large spaces of colour.'

Jack glanced at the painting of an old man traipsing up a mountain with a pack on his back. They were at the Tokyo Art Gallery and he wasn't particularly interested in complex areas or large spaces.

'Mr Doyle,' he said. 'Why are we here?'

'To enjoy the art, of course.'

Jack sighed. 'But shouldn't we be investigating Hodder's murder?' he asked. 'Or trying to work out what the parchment means?'

Mr Doyle patiently led him towards the exit. 'His

murder is best handled by the Tokyo Police,' he said. 'If they ask for help, I will assist, but I have no authority to investigate anything without their consent.'

The detective had already been helpful. It had only taken him a moment to spot a tiny wound on Dr Hodder's left forefinger. Examining the lectern, Mr Doyle had discovered a tiny pin embedded in the timber. The police had since established the pin to be poisonous, and the cause of the doctor's death.

'Any number of people had access to the room prior to the doctor's presentation,' Mr Doyle said. 'There is tight security, but the poisonous pin could have been placed there by a hotel staff member, a delivery person, almost anyone.'

'But why did they do it?'

'No doubt the killer worked for one of the industrialists that Albert spoke of—a Metalist.'

'So now we're dealing with both Nazis and Metalists?'

'It seems so.'

'And the Kusanagi sword?'

Mr Doyle tapped the side of his head. 'Working on it,' he said.

Leaving the art gallery, they boarded a steambus. Jack stared out the window without seeing, his thoughts turning to Scarlet. He couldn't stop thinking about her. Today she had opted to visit a bookstore and buy Japanese copies of the Brinkie Buckeridge books—with Hiro.

'Why do you think Scarlet decided to go out with Hiro today?' Jack asked.

'You know her love of Brinkie Buckeridge,' Mr Doyle said, gently. 'I imagine she wants to purchase a complete set.' He peered at Jack. 'Why do you ask?'

Because I'm worried she's in love with Hiro, he wanted to say. *Or he's in love with her.*

But Scarlet was her own person. Jack couldn't say who she could go out with or not.

'No reason,' he replied.

Mr Doyle, pursing his lips, said nothing.

The steambus crept through the busy metropolis to the hotel. It was late in the day by the time they arrived. Albert Einstein hurried over to them.

'Ignatius,' he said. 'I've been looking for you.'

'What's happened?'

'Firstly, I wanted to apologise.'

'Whatever for?'

'I invited you here as our guest of honour. Instead you've almost been blown up on a space steamer, someone has tried to rob you and we've had a murder.'

Mr Doyle laughed. 'For us,' he said, 'that's nothing unusual.'

Einstein leant close. 'Just between us,' he said, 'it's a terrible tragedy that Dr Hodder was murdered, but he *was* the most boring speaker I've ever heard.'

'I did fall asleep shortly after he started on the Jurassic period.'

'Anyway, there's been some talk of moving the symposium.'

'Where to?'

'That's still being decided,' he said. 'I'll let you know when a plan is made.'

As Einstein headed off, Jack spotted Scarlet and Hiro returning with shopping bags.

'Buying books?' Mr Doyle teased.

'Only the whole Brinkie Buckeridge collection,' she said. 'How often does someone get the opportunity to buy every book—written in Japanese?'

'But you can't read Japanese,' Jack pointed out.

'So?'

They went upstairs. After Scarlet had packed her books away, Mr Doyle produced the parchment and unfurled it on the table. It had no smell, but had an odd texture.

'It's made from goatskin,' Mr Doyle explained. 'Most parchments are made from animal hide, soaked in lime and coated with an egg sealant.'

They had not looked at it since retrieving it from the temple. Clearly it was a map of a bay somewhere, with a nearby mountain.

That could be anywhere, Jack thought.

'It doesn't make any sense.'

Mr Doyle rubbed his chin. 'It is rather odd,' he agreed. 'Let's take it one step at a time.'

'It appears to be part of the coast,' Scarlet said. 'Do you recognise it, Hiro?'

'No,' Hiro said.

'So you don't know of a body of water with a mountain in the middle?' Mr Doyle asked.

'It is not familiar.'

Mr Doyle peered closer. 'There is very little detail here. It could take months—or years—to establish where this is.' He sighed. 'Sometimes it's best to return to basics. What exactly are we looking at?'

'A map of a bay,' Scarlet said. 'And a mountain.'

'And a flower border,' Hiro said.

'Hmm, those are peonies,' Mr Doyle said. 'A very pretty flower.'

'Is there a place that's famous for peonies? And has a mountain?' asked Jack.

Hiro stared at the picture, his brow creasing. 'There is,' he said. 'And that may not be a picture of a mountain, but a volcano. Daikonshima Island was formed by a volcano, and it is famous for its peonies!'

'That must be it!' Scarlet said. 'Is it close by?'

'It will take a few hours to reach by air.'

'I knew something would come to us,' Mr Doyle said. He glanced at his watch. 'It is quite late now. I suggest we retire for the evening and leave first thing in the morning.'

Jack felt like running out the door now and searching for the sword, but he knew what Mr Doyle would say. *Brains and bodies work best when rested.*

Hiro headed back to his aunt, promising to meet them the next day. Scarlet went to her room.

Jack was about to head for his when he saw Mr Doyle grimacing.

'What is it, sir?' he asked.

'It's nothing, really,' he said, 'but my bedroom is directly above the hotel restaurant. The smells at night keep me awake.'

'We can swap rooms, if you like.'

Mr Doyle brightened. 'That would be wonderful,' he said. 'You know what I always say?'

'Er, brains and bodies work best when rested?'

'That's it, Jack.'

Within minutes, Jack was climbing into a different bed and turning out the light.

Mr Doyle was right about the smells from the restaurant. The scent of cooked meat was wafting through the window. But it didn't worry him. He liked meat.

It was many hours later when Jack woke. He glanced at a clock in the corner. 3am. The sounds and smells from the restaurant had faded away, replaced by the faint odour of hot metal and steam.

That's odd, he thought. *It must be coming in from the street.*

He closed his eyes again.

Krrikk!

Lifting his head, Jack saw a gloomy room, illuminated only by light at the window. When he had gone to bed, the window had been open a crack. Now it was wide-open, a gentle breeze shifting the curtain. No-one could have entered the apartment. They were on the sixth floor.

Krrrikkkk!

Jack's heart bulged with fear. *Something* was in the room with him. Reaching over, he grabbed at the table lamp and ignited it.

His mouth fell open in astonishment. A five-foot high mechanical octopus stood in the room, arms weaving about, as if searching. At the end of each arm was a three-pronged claw. Its head was a cylinder with a mechanical eye. No doubt it was very advanced—and equally deadly.

Krrikkk!

Jack peered up to see one of the arms dangling only a few inches over his head. One false move and it would pounce.

I need to create a diversion. But how can I do that without moving?

Jack's eyes spied a book on the bedside table. It was one of Mr Doyle's—*The Great Shadow*—by some British writer, and the pages were fanned open.

Taking a deep breath, Jack carefully blew at the pages. At first nothing happened. Then a few turned.

The mechanical arm whirred and moved towards the book. Jack blew again and the pages flapped more furiously. The claw drew back and slammed into the book, punching a hole right through, just as Jack rolled off the other side of the futon.

Scampering under the mattress, he screamed for help as he levered it upright. The metal monster beat against it, but could not break through.

Jack continued to yell. He heard the bedroom door open.

'Good grief!' Mr Doyle cried.

Jack pushed the futon towards the creature, trying to block its view, but one of its arms slammed the door shut. Only one exit remained—the window.

Diving across the room, Jack proceeded to climb onto the window ledge that ran the length of the building. Heights did not scare him—he had been an acrobat for years—but he preferred the safety of a net.

Edging along as quickly as possible, he heard a shot ring out in his bedroom. And another. There was no mistaking the boom of Mr Doyle's gun. The metal octopus crashed through the window, and landed on the ledge. It paused momentarily, its claws waving about in the air, before turning towards Jack and starting after him.

Bazookas!

Reaching the next window, Jack peered into a hotel hallway. Smashing a pane with his elbow, he shoved the window up and started through until a claw grabbed his leg. He tried to struggle free, but it held him tight.

Blam! Blam! Blam!

Mr Doyle advanced, gun in hand, down the hallway. Scarlet was behind him, gripping a fire axe. The bullets slammed into the machine's body, sending steam escaping.

Jack tried to wrestle free. 'It won't let go,' he gasped.

Mr Doyle fired again and this time something exploded in the machine's torso. Hot metal flew everywhere, and it became a dead weight as it slid backwards through the window, dragging Jack after it.

Throwing himself at Jack, Mr Doyle pinned him

to the ground, but now both of them were being pulled out. Scarlet brought the fire axe down onto the final tentacle gripping Jack's leg. Oil sprayed from the wound.

'Hurry!' Jack yelled.

She brought the axe down a second time, and a third.

Something snapped in the leg and the octopus fell back through the window. A moment later they heard it crash into the street.

Mr Doyle helped Jack up. 'I'm sorry that happened, my boy,' he said. 'That monster could have killed you.'

'Don't blame yourself,' Jack said, rubbing his leg. 'It's not your fault.'

'It partly is,' Mr Doyle said, sheepishly. 'That creature was probably supposed to kill me.'

CHAPTER TEN

The dragonfly zoomed across the sky.

Jack, Scarlet and Mr Doyle huddled together in the cold cabin. They had started early after a restless night's sleep. The police had been called, the machine retrieved and their group moved to another room. Einstein had arrived during the midst of the drama, apologising for the attack.

'The Metalists must be trying to disrupt the conference,' he said to Mr Doyle. 'Killing the guest of honour would severely destroy the reputation of the Darwinist League.'

'I suggest security be bolstered,' Mr Doyle said.

'There are already as many security guards as there

are delegates,' Einstein said. 'But I'll ask the police to send more officers.'

After Einstein had left, Mr Doyle turned to Jack. 'It seems we have landed in the middle of a sticky situation. Someone wants to destroy the Darwinist League, but we have our own enemies trying to stop us from pursuing the Kusanagi sword.'

Hiro spoke over his shoulder. 'You will not give up,' he said. 'Will you?'

'I'm not sure the sword can be found,' Mr Doyle said. 'It may have been destroyed centuries ago. Regardless, I still need to locate my scoundrel step-brother.'

'You call him a scoundrel,' Hiro said. 'But I found him to be very smart.'

'He is smart,' Mr Doyle said. 'He's also one of the most accomplished liars I've ever known.'

Scarlet turned to Jack. 'I've been thinking that I owe you an apology,' she said.

'For what?'

'I doubted that ninjas existed. I even suggested you might have hallucinated that episode with the red ninja. I'm sorry.'

'That's all right.'

Hiro glanced back at them. 'Scarlet told me you met a ninja,' he said. 'A red ninja.'

Jack told him how the woman on the rooftop had saved his life. 'What do you know about her?' he asked.

'The red ninja is legendary,' he explained. 'She helps the poor and fights crime.'

Jack smiled smugly. 'So she is like Ninja Star,' Jack said. 'In *Ninety-Nine Ninjas*, he travels to Britain to save the King of England from being assassinated.'

'Goodness,' Scarlet said. 'He sounds like a Japanese Brinkie Buckeridge.'

'Oh, he's much more talented than Biscuit Budgerigar,' Jack said. 'He only has one arm.'

'One arm? How does he fight evildoers?'

'He's *very* good with his feet.'

After travelling west for hours, they turned south over the sea. Hiro followed the coast until they reached some lakes. The first contained two large islands with a road joining them to the mainland.

Hiro pointed to the closest.

'The small island is Eshima,' he said. 'The larger is Daikonshima.'

He slowed the dragonfly and circled Daikonshima. There were a few huts on it, but it otherwise appeared unoccupied.

'It's very flat,' Jack said.

'I'm not sure where we're going to find a cave,' Scarlet said.

Mr Doyle had been checking the parchment. 'That's the section of coast,' he said, pointing. 'At the southern end.'

Landing the dragonfly, Hiro tied it to a nearby tree and they trekked down to the edge of the bay.

'I don't see a cave anywhere,' Jack said.

The further they traipsed, the more hopeless Jack

felt. He had imagined they would stumble upon a hill with a cave. Instead, it was only open grassland.

'Are we sure that's a cave?' he asked, after they stopped to look at the parchment again. 'It looks more like a hole than a cave.'

'You may be right,' Mr Doyle said. Taking out his goggles, he studied the grassy field. 'What's that over there?'

They headed over to a place where it looked like the grass had been disturbed. Jack peered at one of the rocks. Unlike the others, which were grey, this was rusty red. He hit the rock with his hand and it gave a hollow ring.

'Jack,' Scarlet said. 'I think you've found it.'

'I think Edgar did first,' Jack said.

Mr Doyle pointed at the ground. 'There are some faint footprints in the dirt,' he said. 'I'll wager they're his.'

They levered up the rock to reveal a set of winding stairs. Mr Doyle lit a candle and they descended.

Finally, they reached a narrow tunnel. The candle-light could not penetrate it, so Mr Doyle pulled an ancient torch from a wall and lit it.

At the other end, they reached a perfectly arched cave with ancient Japanese characters carved into the stone walls. The floor was made from long, narrow paving stones. The whole place smelt of mould and stale water.

Mr Doyle pointed at the walls. 'Do you know what that says?' he asked Hiro.

'It is an ancient Buddhist quote. *As soon as we think we are safe, something unexpected happens.*'

Jack pointed to an altar stone on a raised platform at the far end. 'There's a parchment on that altar,' he said, starting towards it.

A groaning came from under the floor.

'Jack!' Mr Doyle said. 'Don't—'

But he was too late. The piece of floor that Jack had stepped on had begun to tilt downwards. Jack jumped onto the stone in front of him. But it soon began rising out of the ground, so he leapt to the next.

'I'm coming for you!' Mr Doyle yelled.

'No!' Jack yelled. 'I'm all right.'

Mr Doyle quickly lit another torch and threw it to Jack. Each block was an enormous half-circle of rock that swivelled on an unseen pivot. Turning back was suicide.

Jack stepped to the next stone. When it started to drop, he jumped onto the next, and the next.

Within seconds he had reached the platform with the raised altar. The stonework here was firm beneath his feet, but the paving behind him continued to turn like cogs in a giant clock. Only when they were at a particular alignment did he catch a glimpse of Mr Doyle and the others.

'It seems the words on the wall were a warning,' Hiro yelled.

'Thanks,' Jack said, sourly. 'That's really helpful.'

'Never fear, my boy,' Mr Doyle called. 'I'm working on a plan.'

Jack studied the parchment. It was a map, similar to the first, but this one clearly showed an island. At one end of it were pictures of stars, and in the midst of these, a sword.

'Jack! How are you faring?'

After describing the picture to the others, he rolled it up and put it in his coat. 'What do you think it means?' he yelled back.

'I have no idea,' Mr Doyle said. 'But we'll worry about that later. The most important thing is getting you back safely.'

That's easier said than done, Jack thought.

The stones were continuing to rotate as the torch grew dimmer by the second. If he didn't get back over the other side soon, he never would.

'Listen to me, Jack,' Mr Doyle called. 'I have worked out the pattern for the return trip, but you must follow it exactly.'

'Whatever you say.'

Mr Doyle called out a complicated routine of stepping forward and backwards to cross the stones. The instructions went on and on. Finally, when Mr Doyle had repeated them three times, Jack was confident he'd understood them.

'I can do this,' Jack called to them. 'But in case I don't make it—'

'You'll make it,' Mr Doyle assured him. 'If you get lost, listen to the sound of my voice. Now, are you ready?'

'Yes.'

'Wait...wait...now!'

Jack stepped onto the first stone. He paused and

stepped onto the second, then the third. Stepping back to the second, he tried to remember what to do next. Was it forwards again? Or backwards?

'Forwards!' Mr Doyle yelled. 'Now back!'

Jack followed his instructions. There was no time to think. He had to blindly follow Mr Doyle's orders or he would die. Finally, his legs shaking, he reached the other side. Everyone threw their arms around him.

'Jack! Thank goodness you're all right!' Scarlet said.

'You kept calm in a difficult situation,' Hiro said. 'Well done.'

The sweat was dripping off Jack and he felt faint. Gripping Mr Doyle's arm, he said, 'I couldn't have done it without you. Thank you, sir.'

The detective said nothing, just gave him another tight hug.

'At least we have the next map,' Jack said, showing them the parchment. 'What do you think it means?'

After staring at it in silence for a moment, Mr Doyle slowly shook his head. 'I have no idea,' he said. 'It's as incomprehensible as the first.'

CHAPTER ELEVEN

'Have you decided what seminar you'll be attending today?' Einstein asked.

Jack, Scarlet and Mr Doyle were sitting in the hotel's restaurant. They had returned the previous day and pored over the parchment for hours without success. It seemed to be a picture of an island, but there were thousands of islands surrounding Japan. It could take years to find the right one.

So Mr Doyle had suggested they attend some more seminars. They had to keep up appearances that they were only in Japan for the symposium, anyway.

'Perhaps,' Mr Doyle said to Einstein. 'The one about making sheep as big as steamcars sounds fascinating.'

'So does the one about increasing the brain capacity of chimps,' Scarlet said, staring at the program. 'Is this really true? That someone believes a chimp could be made as intelligent as a person?'

'Some chimps are already *more* intelligent than people,' Einstein said. 'A few politicians, for example.'

They all laughed.

Suddenly there was a ruckus from outside the hotel, and a group of policemen entered the lobby. The officer in charge spoke quickly to the desk clerk, who pushed through the seated diplomats and scientists and came towards Einstein.

After introducing himself as Endo, he said, 'We must secure the building immediately. The police have informed us that a protest march is coming this way.'

'Why would that concern us?'

'The marchers are protesting against the Darwinist League.'

Einstein quickly began spreading the word to the other tables as the police secured the building.

'We had best postpone the seminars until we know what's happening,' he said.

'As you say,' Mr Doyle sighed, turning to Jack and Scarlet. 'I suggest ordering some morning tea to be delivered to our room.'

Back in the room, Jack peered out their window at the street below. The police had surrounded the building, but there was no sign of any protesters.

Maybe they've given up and gone home?

After their tea arrived, another knock came at the door.

'They must have forgotten something,' Scarlet said, opening the door. 'Oh, you're not—'

'Forgive me, *fräulein*,' a man with a thick German accent said, pushing into the room. 'The time has come for us to speak.'

'Who are you?' Mr Doyle demanded. 'What are you—?'

The detective stopped. The man in the doorway had thinning black hair, parted to one side, a thick moustache and round-rimmed glasses.

'Allow me to introduce myself,' the man said.

'I know who you are,' Mr Doyle said. 'You're Anton Drexler.'

Jack stared at him. The Nazi leader's picture had been in newspapers ever since his party had triumphed in the recent elections.

But his photograph had not done him justice. In the flesh, his eyes were strangely cold, like those of a dead fish.

Drexler smiled without humour. 'It seems my fame has preceded me,' he said, indicating a seat. 'May I?'

Mr Doyle nodded.

'I will get to the point,' Drexler said. 'You know we are seeking the same prize.'

'And what would that be?'

'You should not play the fool, Herr Doyle. It does not suit you.'

'And if our goals are the same?'

'There can be only one winner,' Drexler said, sitting back in the chair. 'That will be us.'

'What makes you think that?'

'We are stronger, better organised and prepared to do anything to retrieve the sword. You are an old man—like your British empire—a product of a bygone era.' Drexler spread his arms. 'Let me speak to you as a friend.'

Mr Doyle said nothing.

'You have already fought in a war,' Drexler said. 'You know the hardships it brings, the tragedies. How much better if our nations could be at peace?'

'I doubt the Nazi idea of peace is the same as our own.'

'Give me the map to the sword and we can part as friends.'

'We will never be friends.'

'Germany was defeated in the last war,' Drexler said. 'But our glorious nation will rise again and the German people will live out its true destiny, as the masters of Europe. Once we recover the sword and present it to the Japanese government, an alliance will be formed that will shake the world.'

'Most people in Germany and Japan want to live happy, peaceful lives,' Mr Doyle said. 'You're a small man who talks big. You speak of master races and global domination, but my admiration lies with men and women who work hard to raise their children, nourish them with love and kindness, and peacefully live with their neighbours to make better communities and—ultimately—a better world.'

Drexler's face blackened. 'You're a fool!' he snapped. 'When the next war begins—and there will be another war—I will personally make certain you and everyone you hold dear is annihilated. History will remember you as a failure!'

'I'll let history make its own judgements.'

Drexler leapt to his feet, fury in his eyes. 'You will be sorry we ever met!'

'I already am. You're a cockroach. Now leave before I crush you underfoot.'

Drexler stormed out of the room, slamming the door behind.

Jack and Scarlet stared at Mr Doyle. 'What are we going to do?' Jack asked.

'Order a new pot of tea,' Mr Doyle said. 'This one has gone quite cold.'

'Mr Doyle!' Scarlet said. 'That man has threatened to destroy us.'

'Then we will be careful.' He tilted his head. 'What is that sound?'

Racing to the window, they saw a large crowd, carrying banners and chanting, had approached the hotel.

'It looks like the protesters have arrived,' Mr Doyle said. 'I suggest we go downstairs in case things turn nasty.'

By the time they reached the foyer, the cries of the protesters had risen to a roar. Hundreds of people now surrounded the building. The hotel staff had bolted all the doors. Einstein and Dr Livanov were speaking to a police officer.

'May I ask what's happening?' Mr Doyle inquired.

'This appears to have been a well-orchestrated protest by Metalists,' Einstein said. 'Clearly they want to disrupt the symposium and discredit our work.'

A smash came from the other end of the lobby as a rock crashed through a window. The police chief raced off, yelling orders. Then a Molotov cocktail smashed through a window in the dining room and exploded. The screams of the crowd became more frenzied.

'This is out of control,' Mr Doyle said. 'It's become a fully fledged riot!'

Jack, Scarlet and Mr Doyle ran to the fire. There was no water around, so they snatched up tablecloths to beat it out as Einstein raced up to them.

'This is getting worse by the minute,' he said. 'Another fire's broken out on the other side.'

'Are the fire brigade coming?' Mr Doyle asked.

'They're already here, but they can't get through the crowd.'

As they followed Einstein back through the lobby, one of the main windows shattered and people with signs burst through.

Jack and the others were surrounded in seconds. Mr Doyle was hit over the head with a sign, and Scarlet punched the perpetrator in the face. Einstein fought bravely against two assailants as a lobby boy came to his aid.

Then police officers arrived, driving back the protesters.

Endo raced over. 'We're evacuating the hotel. There's an exit out the back. I suggest you use it.'

Another flaming torch was thrown through a window. A fire alarm began to ring and guests came streaming down the stairs, many of them lugging bags. Staff started directing them towards the rear of the building.

Following them, Jack suddenly slapped his pockets in alarm.

Oh no, he thought. *My compass and picture are still in our apartment!*

It would only take him a minute to grab them.

Breaking away from the group, he raced upstairs. He reached their rooms and scooped the items off his dressing table as more crashes came from below. Either the protesters were causing more havoc, or the fire was really taking hold.

Jack hurried down the hall and pushed the elevator button, but remembered that the stairs should always be used in a fire. They were already empty of people. With all the smoke, it was getting harder to breath by the second. Reaching the fire doors, he felt a wall of heat behind them.

What's going on?

He pushed one open a crack—and cried out. Beyond lay a wall of fire. It had only taken minutes, but the fire was completely out of control.

The hotel was burning to the ground with him in it.

CHAPTER TWELVE

Clouds of smoke chasing him, Jack staggered up the stairs. He had to get out of here, but the only way to do that was from the roof. Things were popping and exploding downstairs as sirens filled the air: fire brigades were arriving. The hotel alarm bell was ringing, but then it ominously cut out.

It was getting hotter by the minute. Jack had been in burning buildings before, but he had never seen a structure catch fire so quickly. Then he remembered: *This whole place is made from timber.*

Racing up the remaining five floors to the roof, he ran to the edge, but was alarmed to see flames already billowing up that side of the building.

Bazookas, he thought. *I'm going to get fried like a sausage!*

The building groaned alarmingly beneath him. Glancing over the edge, he saw the rioters had withdrawn. A fire engine was ineffectually hosing down the structure, but it was too little, too late. The fire had already spread to an adjoining building. This was turning into a major catastrophe.

He looked upwards at the sky above. For once, it was clear of dragonflies.

You can never get a lift when you need one!

Police had formed a roadblock further down the street where Mr Doyle was struggling to get through. Scarlet spotted Jack and waved in alarm. In London, there were airships that could put out fires, but they obviously didn't have them here in Japan. He had to get off this roof, but how?

Clunk!

Jack turned in alarm. A grappling hook, attached to a rope, had wrapped around a chimney behind him. It led to a figure on the roof of the next building.

The red ninja!

She pulled the rope tight and tied her end to a pole on her building as the crackling of the fire grew louder. The flames were only two storeys below and would reach Jack within seconds.

Gripping the rope, he pulled himself headfirst over the edge and lifted his legs up so his ankles crossed over the rope. He started dragging himself across to the ninja's building. He'd done this a hundred times at the circus, but not without a net, and not ten storeys above the ground. The flames from the fire began licking the rope as a huge crash came from below. If he didn't reach the other side soon—

A hand gripped his shoulder, and Jack looked up into the eyes of the red ninja. He had reached the other side.

Untangling himself from the rope, Jack glanced back to the hotel. It was fully alight, and wouldn't have held for much longer. When he went to thank the ninja, she was gone.

'What is this woman?' Jack asked. 'Invisible?'

Within seconds, he was back on the street and racing towards the barriers. Mr Doyle and Scarlet appeared.

'What happened?' Mr Doyle asked. 'We turned around and you were gone. The police wouldn't let us back in the building.'

When Jack explained he had gone back for his belongings, Mr Doyle's face darkened.

'My boy,' he said. 'I know they're precious to you, but they don't equal a human life.' His eyes glistening, he pulled Jack close. 'Especially yours.'

'I'm sorry, Mr Doyle.'

'Jack,' Scarlet said, gently touching his arm. 'I suppose you wanted to save my Brinkie Buckeridge books too.'

'Er, no. I forgot about them.'

'Oh.'

Two buildings were now fully alight. Jack and the

others were forced back to another barrier as a dozen fire engines worked to contain the flames. The ground shook when the hotel collapsed.

Jack stared at the scene in disbelief. An hour before, they had been comfortably settled into the hotel. Now it was a smouldering ruin.

Checking his pockets, Jack gripped the locket and the compass. Mr Doyle was right to be angry. He shouldn't have risked his life to save them.

Red faced and puffing, Hiro appeared. 'I could see the fire from a mile away,' he said. 'I am pleased you are all safe.'

'Me too,' Jack said.

Einstein also appeared. 'I'm so glad you're all fine,' he said. 'We're reassembling at a *ryokan* down the block.'

'We're not going to a hotel?' Jack said.

'It's an inn,' Mr Doyle explained. 'Dating back to the seventeenth century, they were originally situated on highways for travellers.'

Leaving the sound of fire engines behind them, they made their way down the block, reaching a timber clad two-storey building called the *Utsukushii*. A large pool took up most of the reception area with paintings of ancient Japanese buildings lining the walls.

Livanov was pointing people to a function room at the back. When all of the scientists and diplomats had assembled, she stepped onto a stage and called for silence. 'I'm pleased to report that everyone at the hotel survived the fire,' she said. 'We can thank the staff for their speedy action in getting everyone out.

'I know this has been a terrible setback. The police arrested a number of protesters, but they have refused to speak. It seems clear, however, that the demonstration was initiated by a supporter of the Metalists, possibly an industrialist here in Japan.'

'What will happen now?' the diplomat from France asked. 'Surely we must abandon the symposium?'

'That's exactly what we must *not* do,' Livanov said. 'The Hot Earth crisis is the most serious threat to ever face mankind. The accord must be signed this week, or it will be too late.'

'But Hodder has already been killed!' a scientist protested. 'And we've lost all our belongings!'

Angry murmuring broke out among the crowd. People started to walk out.

Einstein took to the stage. 'I understand your concerns,' he said. 'But a backup plan has already been established.'

'You mean there's somewhere we can move?' a woman asked.

'Indeed. We had already anticipated problems in case there was an issue with the hotel.'

One of the diplomats raised his hand. 'Where are we moving?' he asked. 'And is it safe?'

Einstein was able to manage a smile. 'Is it safe?' he asked. 'Not only is it made to keep people out, but also to keep them in!'

An hour later, the members of the symposium were

moving into their new accommodation.

'Well, I must admit,' Mr Doyle said. 'It certainly looks secure.'

They were standing in the courtyard of the old Tokyo jail, which comprised half-a-dozen stone buildings surrounding a courtyard. The prisoners had been recently transferred to a new modern facility on the city outskirts, and the old building converted into a modern hotel. It was so new, in fact, that scaffolds still lined some walls while several of the rooms had not been painted.

The scientists were housed in one building, with the diplomats and their staff in another. Jack and the others had another wing to themselves.

On the way to their new accommodation, they had gone out to buy some essentials: a few changes of clothing and toiletries. Jack had a small cell with a comfortable bed, with Mr Doyle across the hall and Scarlet in a room at the other end.

It was now late in the day. Mr Doyle suggested they eat a meal and get a good night's sleep.

The next morning Jack joined Mr Doyle and Scarlet in the jail's dining room, enjoying a bowl of soup and omelette.

They met Hiro in the foyer of the jail.

'What will we do today?' Jack asked.

'There's a session on improving Milverton's Terrafirma,' Mr Doyle said, peering at an agenda on the wall. 'And another about building houses from the calcium carbonate of starfish.'

Hiro's eyes shone with excitement. 'Starfish,' he said. 'I think I have it.'

'What?' Jack said.

'I may know where the map is leading us. For hundreds of years, Hoshizuna-no-hama beach has been famous for its star-shaped sand. It is a remote island far to the south-west of Japan.'

'So the sand is shaped like stars?' Jack asked.

'In truth, the sand is not. The grains are actually the skeletons of tiny sea creatures.'

Mr Doyle nodded thoughtfully. 'This fits with the images on the parchment,' Mr Doyle said. 'I suggest we go there, but first we should pick up diving and camping supplies.'

'I know a shop,' Hiro said. 'My parents and I used to go there when I was young.'

After picking up their equipment, they started on the long journey over Japan.

'Will this take long?' Jack asked.

'Most of the day,' Hiro replied. 'I advise you to get some sleep.'

Jack nodded, closing his eyes. When he opened them again, they were flying over sparkling water and the sun was low in the sky.

'Are we there yet?' he asked Hiro.

'Almost,' Hiro said.

I hope this leads to something, Jack thought. *Otherwise it will have been a complete waste of our time.*

Glancing at Mr Doyle and Scarlet, Jack thought

they looked as exhausted as he felt. The detective's eyes were closed; he was either asleep or meditating, while Scarlet was reading a book. Noticing he was awake, she put it down.

'Sleep well?' she asked.

'More or less.'

'You should read for a while.'

'I lost my book in the fire.'

'You should have told me,' Scarlet said, producing another book from a pocket in her dress. 'It's one of my favourites—*The Adventure of the Stolen Face*.'

'The Stolen Face?' Jack stared at her. 'Really?'

'It's a complex mystery where Brinkie investigates a series of murders where the victims' faces have been stolen.'

'It sounds terrifying.'

'It is, although in some cases it's an improvement.'

As Scarlet continued, Jack wondered again about her and Hiro. She had an oddly wistful look in her eye. Had anything happened between the two while he'd slept? Jack had never told Scarlet how he felt about her.

Maybe I've left it too late, he thought. *I should have said something.*

'...and you'll never guess what Brinkie does in the end,' Scarlet said.

'What?'

'She disables the bomb using only a banana. Isn't that incredible?'

'We should all carry one—just in case.'

Hiro interrupted them. 'We're almost there,' he said.

Mr Doyle stirred himself and they all peered over Hiro's shoulder at a group of islands. Hiro pointed to a large square-shaped island to the west.

'That's Iriomote-jima.'

Sunlight sparkled off the shimmering water as they came in low over the beach and settled onto the sand.

A flock of brightly coloured birds flew away in panic as they disembarked from the dragonfly. Jack's back ached from the long journey. The egg-shaped cabin was fine for short flights, but too confined for long journeys.

Looking around, Jack saw a rock platform clung to one end of the beach with a series of small islands at the other. Thick vegetation crowded the interior. A warm breeze swept across the beach. Despite the dramas of the last few days, Jack couldn't help but relax.

'Is Hoshizuna-no-hama populated?' Mr Doyle asked.

'Only by a few people,' Hiro said. 'Supply ships service these islands monthly.'

The sun was now straddling the far horizon.

'We had best make camp,' Mr Doyle said. 'Tomorrow will be a big day.'

It only took a few minutes to unpack the vessel. Mr Doyle pulled out the tents. They were made of a super-thin material, designed by the Darwinists, and silver-coloured.

'Apparently it's derived from spider's web,' Mr Doyle said. 'Virtually unbreakable.'

The scuba tanks—single torpedo-shaped cylinders

filled with compressed air—and goldfish bowl helmets were left onboard the dragonfly, as they wouldn't be needed until the next day.

The wind began to turn cool as the sky darkened. Jack suspected it would get cold later. After making a fire, Hiro chopped up assorted vegetables at lightning speed and was serving a meal within minutes.

'You're so fast,' Jack said.

'My parents taught me to prepare meals from when I was very young,' Hiro explained. 'They both worked a lot.'

'So you didn't have many holidays?'

'We used to go camping. There was a park ground we visited a lot. They were killed in an accident when I was young.'

'You must miss them,' Jack said. He told Hiro about the incident involving his own parents. 'It's hard to lose someone you're close to.'

'I don't remember them very well,' Hiro said. 'It happened when I was five. After their deaths I went to live with my aunt and uncle, who owned a clothing factory and taught me everything about their business.'

'Why aren't you working there now?' Mr Doyle asked.

'The business failed.' Hiro did not speak for some time, swallowing hard. 'A local crime boss tried to extort money from them, but they would not pay.

'One day, after working with my uncle at the factory, I went home to help my aunt make dinner. I still remember what we cooked: grilled salmon and vegetables. At first I thought uncle was running late. Putting the meal in the oven to keep it warm, I read a book and waited.'

Hiro paused. Jack watched the boy's haunted eyes in the dim light. He looked almost like a different person.

'My aunt finally pointed out how late it was,' Hiro said. 'I'll never forget looking at my watch and the terrible shock I felt when I realised the time. I knew something was wrong. I ran from the house. The roads were congested and it took me almost an hour to get to our factory. When I arrived it was completely dark.

'My uncle's body was lying behind his desk. He had been shot by the crime boss. In his hand...' Hiro swallowed hard. 'There was a small picture frame in his hand. After he was shot, I think he was able to drag himself to his desk and grasp it. It was a family picture of us all.'

'What did the police do?' Jack asked.

'They were being bribed.' Hiro sighed. 'After my uncle was killed, my aunt tried to continue the business, but the workers were afraid for their own lives and left.'

'I'm sorry to hear that,' Jack said, gently. 'And you now make your living as a guide?'

'It's good money,' Hiro said, not meeting their eyes. 'One day I will have my own business.'

'I'm sure you will.'

Finishing their meal, they washed up and went to their tents.

Jack lay in his sleeping bag, watching the wind blow

against the tent's walls. He felt bad for Hiro.

We have a lot in common, he thought. *Not only have we both lost our parents, but we're in love with the same girl.*

Turning his head, Jack looked through a tiny gauze window at the darkened ocean. Tokyo was very distant, and London even further. He thought about the visit from Anton Drexler. What had the man said?

When the next war begins—and there will be another war—I will personally make certain you and everyone you hold dear is annihilated.

Jack shuddered. *What a terrible man.*

Closing his eyes, Jack slept, but his dreams were unsettled. He found himself on a battlefield, surrounded by trenches. It was dusk and clouds were scudding across the horizon. Men lay dying all around. Some had been shot. Others had been blown up.

A series of artillery shots exploded on the horizon. Jack stared at them in fascination before realising they were drawing nearer. He ran, but the explosions continued to grow louder. Reaching the top of a hill, Jack saw a fire had started on the battlefield, enveloping everything in its path.

I can't get away, he thought. *It's moving too fast.*

He looked down. A blanket and a sword had mysteriously appeared at his feet. *I can use the blanket to fight back the fire.* The flames had reached the bottom of the hill and were now racing up on all sides, consuming everything in their path.

Jack beat them back with the blanket, but within seconds the material had begun to smoulder. He dropped the blanket as the flames surrounded him.

It's not working, he thought. *I'm going to die.*

Then Jack looked across at another hill. At the top stood a small man—Hikaru Satou. The old man nodded sagely at him.

Hesitantly, Jack picked up the sword.

There is a gap between knowing and science.

His hands shook as he raised it overhead.

The Kusanagi Sword can only be wielded by one who is true of heart and believes in its power.

The sword began to glow.

CHAPTER THIRTEEN

'Jack?'

Opening his eyes, Jack saw Scarlet's head poking in the door of his tent.

'Wake up, sleepyhead,' she said. 'We're having a cup of tea before we go diving.'

Outside, the sun had just risen and the sky was similar to that in his dream. Scarlet had said that dreams sometimes revealed things from a person's subconscious.

'What do you think it all means?' he asked her, after explaining the dream.

'I'm not sure,' Scarlet said. 'It sounds like a mishmash of things: the visit from that horrible man, Drexler, the possibility of another war, and the visit to Mr Satou's garden.'

Mr Doyle had already begun preparing the diving gear.

'Have you ever dived before?' he asked them.

Hiro had many times, but it was new to Jack and Scarlet. Mr Doyle explained how the system worked. The metal and glass helmet screwed onto a canvas suit. A pipe ran from the oxygen tank, worn like a backpack, to a flange at the back of the helmet. Mr Doyle pointed at weights on the belt.

'These will take us down to the bottom,' he said.

'And to get back up?' Jack asked.

'This is a buoyancy control bag,' Mr Doyle explained, pointing at an odd sack on the side. 'It's a bladder that fills with air that will gradually allow us to ascend.'

They all went to get changed. After clambering into his gear, Jack emerged to find Mr Doyle waiting, staring out at the sea.

'Mr Doyle,' he said.

'I'm sorry, my boy,' he said. 'I was just thinking about the possibility of another war.'

'Do you think it'll happen?'

'The last war is still fresh in people's minds. Most people will do whatever they can to avoid another.'

Scarlet and Hiro climbed from their tents. Hiro pointed at the bottom of Mr Doyle's suit.

'You have a problem with your suit,' he said.

Mr Doyle cursed. 'This is torn,' he said, showing

them a rip in one of the legs. 'Dash it all. I'll need to repair it before I can go down.'

He searched the vessel but ten minutes later returned, frowning.

'The repair kit's not there,' he said.

Hiro looked distressed. 'I should have checked the equipment,' he said. 'This is my fault.'

'Don't be too hard on yourself,' Mr Doyle consoled him. 'But I'm not sure what we'll do.'

'Hiro and I can still do down,' Jack said.

'We *all* can,' Scarlet said, elbowing Jack.

'I'm not sure—'

'We'll have Hiro with us,' Scarlet said. 'He's done lots of diving. And it means there are three of us if we get into trouble.'

The detective still looked uncertain.

'Mr Doyle,' Jack said. 'We've come all this way. We can't turn back now.'

Grudgingly, Mr Doyle agreed, but he made them promise to be careful.

'Have you ever known me to take a risk?' Jack asked.

The detective harrumphed. Then, leading them to the water's edge, he said, 'The map is sparse on detail. The next clue is somewhere off shore, but you'll have to search a large area. There's only three hour's worth of air in your tanks.'

'We'll divide the bottom into a grid,' Hiro said. 'After walking the length of the seabed, parallel to the beach, we'll head out another twenty feet, turn and

return to the starting point. Then we will repeat that until we find the clue.'

Wading into the water, Hiro told Jack and Scarlet to duck their heads and test the gear. Jack found himself peering at a strange underwater world where the visibility faded after twenty feet.

How will we find the next clue?

Lifting his head, he spotted Mr Doyle on the shore. The detective gave him a wave and mouthed something. *Be careful.* Jack nodded.

He swam after Hiro and Scarlet as the sandbar gradually dropped away. As the water got deeper, it grew clearer, and Jack could see an underwater terrain of sandy hills about fifty feet down. The distant sun cut channels of light through the misty water, reflecting off a school of silver fish that stopped to look at them before darting away.

After a minute, Hiro signalled for them to stop. They turned left and walked three abreast along the length of the sand, then did a U-turn to return.

Jack checked his air tank. He still had over two hours.

They continued combing the seabed. Just as he was beginning to think they would never find anything, he saw a rocky outcrop with a dark shadow underneath.

He signalled the others and they swam to it. The shadow proved to be a tunnel, wide enough for the three of them. The tunnel curved around, heading back towards the island. Soon the light had dimmed to almost nothing.

We're back under the island again, Jack thought. *We'll be in darkness soon.*

Just then, he saw a faint glow ahead, like a distant star. Jack's head broke the surface and he found himself in a pool adjacent to an underground stone room with a timber door at the far end. It was so dark it was almost impossible to see anything. The only light entering was through a tiny circular hole in the ceiling.

They removed their diving gear. The floor was ankle-deep in old leaves and the air smelt musty.

'We're under the island,' Jack said. 'That hole must be a location that's impossible for people to reach, so they've never seen this room.'

'But what is it?' Scarlet said, peering about.

'I don't know,' Hiro replied. 'It is not a temple—or not like any temple I have ever seen.'

'There's markings on that door,' Scarlet said. 'Let's take a closer look.'

As they started forward, a small alarm went off in the back of Jack's mind. 'Maybe we should wait—'

But he was too late.

Boom!

A stone wall slammed into place behind them.

Hiro pointed to the walls on each side. 'They are moving!' he cried.

Jack went to the door. It was solid, made of camphor. 'There are engravings on here,' he said. 'Some kind of picture.'

Scarlet's mouth fell open. 'Yes!' she cried, clapping

her hands together with excitement. 'This has never happened before!'

'What?' Jack said.

'The converging walls! It happens in almost every Brinkie Buckeridge novel. She enters a room and the walls start to move in from both sides, threatening to crush her to a pulp!'

'I'm so glad you're pleased. So how do we get out of here?'

'The picture must be a puzzle. Solving it will open the door.'

'And if we don't?'

'Then we'll all end up a lot skinnier.'

They frantically examined the engravings. A winding line ran from the top of the door to the bottom with six horizontal lines dividing it into twelve sections. An image of a man, fox, bird and pile of beans was in the top left corner, and the same in the bottom right. The pictures were repeated on timber buttons in each of the squares.

Jack groaned. 'What does it mean?' he asked, eyeing the converging walls. They would meet in a matter of minutes.

'I don't know,' Scarlet said. 'It's never this hard in the books.'

Jack turned to Hiro. 'What do you think?'

'We may be in luck,' Hiro said, thoughtfully. 'This is an ancient puzzle. There have been many variations over the years, but here is the essence of it: a farmer has to transport a fox, bird and beans across the river.'

A trickle of sweat ran down Jack's face as the walls continued to converge.

'So?' he said. 'That's easy enough.'

'Except he can only transport one item at a time. If he takes the fox, the bird will be left behind and eat the beans. If he takes the beans, the fox will eat the bird.'

'All right. So he just needs to take the bird across first, then the fox...' He stopped. 'Oh, that would leave the fox and bird together while he goes back for the beans.'

The walls were now about five feet apart.

'Yes,' Hiro agreed. 'It is very puzzling.'

'So how is it solved?' Jack asked.

'I don't remember.'

'*You don't remember?*'

'Don't blame Hiro,' Scarlet scolded Jack. 'I don't see you coming up with an answer.'

You're only defending him because he's your boyfriend, Jack thought.

'Wait!' Hiro said. 'I know what to do.' He pointed at the figures. 'The farmer takes the bird, then the beans, but then he returns the bird and takes the fox back.'

Scarlet shrieked. 'And then he comes back for the bird!'

'Yes!' Jack yelled. 'That's it!'

The walls were almost upon them. Hiro pushed the buttons, representing the paths of the bird, beans and fox. The walls stopped and the door clicked open.

'That was much easier than in *The Adventure of the Squashed Guide*,' Scarlet said.

They stepped through.

'What on earth—' Jack started.

A cavern lay ahead, lit by another circular hole in the middle of the roof. At its centre was a stone column surrounded by a spidery wooden structure. Timber posts speared up from the ground and intersected with planks that ran from one to another. A few ladders led to the tops of other poles. Half-a-dozen skeletons lay scattered around the floor.

'I don't think we're the first ones here,' Jack said.

'I think you're right,' Scarlet said.

A click came from behind as the door shut. Jack tried reopening it, but there was no handle.

'So we're trapped here,' he said.

'This cannot be a dead end,' Hiro said. 'Finding the parchment must lead us out.'

'But how do we do that?' Scarlet asked, looking at the strange construction in the middle of the cavern. 'What is that thing?'

'An obstacle course,' Jack said. He pointed to the stone column in the middle. 'I'd be willing to bet the next clue is at the top of that.'

'You're probably right, but it doesn't look easy to get to.'

'I can do it,' Hiro said.

Jack felt a flush of anger. 'Don't be ridiculous!' he snapped. 'I used to be an acrobat in a circus. What experience do you have climbing around like a monkey?'

Hiro pursed his lips. 'I was just offering,' he said.

'It appears very dangerous.'

'As if I can't see that!' Jack forced himself to be calm. Yelling at Hiro wouldn't achieve anything. 'I appreciate the offer, but you wouldn't survive five minutes up there.'

'That ladder,' Scarlet said, 'is furthest from the centre, but it seems to be the only way to get to the middle. The hardest part will be the standalone posts.'

Jack nodded. The posts *were* scary. Spearing straight up from the floor, he'd have to move from one to the next much like stepping stones to cross a river.

'I think you're right,' Hiro said.

'Jack,' Scarlet said. 'Are you sure you want to do this?'

'We haven't come this far to give up now.'

He climbed the wooden ladder. *How old is this thing*, he wondered. *A thousand years?* He noticed his hands were shaking.

Swallowing hard, Jack forced himself to climb. At the top, he took a deep breath as he walked across a plank that led to a pole.

His heart was beating hard, but he knew he had to remain calm. *Panicking won't help*. A plank overhead stretched across to another post. Gripping this, he edged himself across, landing nimbly on the top of a white post.

I'm almost there, he thought. *Just a few more—*

Suddenly the post swung wildly to the left. Jack bit back a cry as he was forced to step to another on his right, leaving the first to swing back to its original position. Glancing down, he saw two skeletons below.

So that's what happened to them.

The white post was now out of reach. Going back was not an option, but now he was stranded tantalisingly close to the final stone column. There was another post in front, but stepping to it would still leave him six feet from the column. Giving up seemed to be the only option. He would have to use the post to slide down to the ground, but it was a long way and he'd be lucky not to break something.

'Jack,' Hiro's voice came from below. 'You must stay calm.'

That's easy for you to say!

'I am,' Jack said. 'Does anyone have any ideas?'

Silence. He experimentally placed a foot on the next post. It was solid, but still six feet from the main column. But there was a parchment, he could just glimpse it—on top of the pillar. But Jack still couldn't make out the images.

I've come a long way, he thought. *But not far enough!*

A sound came from behind. 'Jack?'

It was Hiro. 'Are you insane?' Jack hissed. Hiro had followed the obstacle course and made it as far as the first of the twelve steps. 'How did you do that?'

'I used to climb a lot as a boy. I believe there is a way to do this, but we must work as a team. Can we do that?'

'Of course.'

'Are you sure?'

Jack stared into Hiro's eyes. He had to put away his feelings of jealousy if they stood any chance of making this work. 'Yes,' he said. 'I'm positive.'

'Good.' Hiro explained his plan.

'Hiro,' Jack said, when he had finished. 'That's insane.'

'We can do this.'

Sighing, Jack moved to the next post, as Hiro crossed to the post Jack had just vacated. Jack locked his fingers together. 'I'm ready,' he said. 'But this is still madness.'

'It is sometimes a mad world.'

Hiro stepped onto Jack's interlocked hands, and Jack propelled him towards the stone column where Hiro grabbed the top edge. Now Jack was completely off balance—but that was part of the plan. Still hanging onto Hiro's feet, Jack allowed himself to fall towards the column.

Thwak!

Hiro grunted. 'Now climb up my body,' he instructed.

Jack didn't need to be told twice. Within seconds he had used Hiro as a makeshift ladder to reach the top, pulling Hiro up after him.

Wiping sweat from his face, Jack realised he was not only shaking badly, but was so dizzy he wanted to vomit.

'Jack?' Hiro said.

'I'm all right. Just give me a minute.'

Taking a few deep breaths, the dizziness slowly faded. It was only now he was able to look more closely at the parchment.

'But it's not actually a parchment,' he said.

'They're carvings on the raised rock,' Hiro confirmed. 'Since we can't move it, me must memorise them.'

There were three images: a bird in flight, a perfect circle and a Japanese character.

'They're simple enough to remember,' Jack said. 'But how will we get down from here?'

'That will be easy. The column is sinking.'

Jack looked down. He hadn't noticed they were slowly dropping down into the floor.

A minute later it reached ground level and they walked back to Scarlet, who had been waiting anxiously on the other side.

'Don't ever do that to me again!' she snapped. 'Either of you!'

'Do what?' Jack asked.

Scarlet hit him.

There was a click, and the doors behind them swung open again.

'It looks like we're allowed to go,' Hiro said.

They donned their diving gear, re-entered the water and minutes later emerged on the beach to find Mr Doyle waiting.

'Whatever happened to you?' he cried. 'I was worried sick!'

'We are fine, Mr Doyle,' Hiro said.

'But we found out that Hiro can probably compete in the next Olympics,' Jack said.

Hiro stifled a smile. 'I'd forgotten how much I loved

climbing trees,' he said.

'We discovered the next clue,' Scarlet told Mr Doyle.

Jack described the pictures. Mr Doyle took out a piece of paper and Hiro drew the images. He then pointed at the Japanese character. 'That means *inside*,' he said.

'Inside,' Mr Doyle mused. 'So we have all the pieces of the clue.'

'Now we just need to work out what they mean,' Jack said.

CHAPTER FOURTEEN

'If you haven't been amazed already,' Einstein said, 'I'm sure you'll be astonished by what we have on this afternoon.'

Jack was beginning to feel that he'd had about all the astonishment he could take. He was exhausted: the last thing he wanted was to sit in a room listening to scientists.

Half an hour later, he and the others were in a seminar in what used to be the prison chapel. A scientist by the name of Dr Hardy was describing the latest advancements made in deep-sea diving.

'The jellyfish can swim to great depths without being crushed by the water pressure,' he said. 'It truly is a miracle of evolution—and now we have engineered our very own jellyfish diving suits.'

Hardy pointed to a chart.

'We have made a number of alterations to its anatomy,' he said. 'The first is its size. The creature is now so large that it encompasses a fully grown man, protecting him from the crushing pressure at great depths.'

'The suit has a breathing tube that, when placed in a human mouth, instinctively searches for the trachea. It then synthesizes oxygen from the water that it delivers to the wearer.

'And, finally, we have added an enzyme that allows the wearer to see in virtual darkness. Light penetration decreases substantially the deeper one goes. The jellysuit allows the wearer to see at any depth.'

Jack glanced at Scarlet. She had turned green.

'Are you all right?' he asked.

'Not really,' Scarlet confessed. 'I choked on a piece of apple when I was a child and I've had a phobia ever since about things being stuck in my throat.'

One of the scientists spoke up. 'Can we really trust a creature as inhuman as a jellyfish?' he asked.

'Actually,' Hardy said, 'we've found that a symbiotic relationship is created between the diver and the creature. It's both a blessing and a curse. The jellysuit "bonds" with the diver, and oxygen is transported more effectively with each use. But there is a downside. We've found that only one person can wear the same suit – it won't work on different people.'

As the talk concluded, Hardy received a standing ovation. Jack walked from the chapel with images flashing in his head. *A person can dive to any part of the ocean.*

He tugged at Mr Doyle's arm. 'Just think,' he said. 'People will be able to breathe like fish.'

Mr Doyle nodded. 'It's truly incredible,' he said. 'This biomechanical revolution will change the world. I can see why the Metalists have been so intent on stopping the Darwinists.'

They made their way back to their rooms. Under most circumstances, Jack would have found them gloomy, but now he couldn't stop thinking about diving to the bottom of the ocean.

It was now evening and Mr Doyle suggested skipping dinner in favour of an early night.

Before going to his room, Jack found himself cornered by Scarlet. She had a couple of books in her arms.

'I bought you a present,' she said.

'*Ninety-Nine Ninjas!*' Jack exclaimed.

'It's to replace the copy you lost in the fire.'

Jack looked at the cover of the second book. '*The Adventure of the Talking Cat*,' he read.

'It opens with a wonderful battle scene,' Scarlet said, 'where Brinkie is about to be killed by a four-armed gorilla. She is saved at the last moment by Mr Fluffypants.'

'Mr Fluffypants?'

'Her cat,' Scarlet explained. 'Named after her great uncle Ebenezer Fluffypants.'

Thanking her again, Jack staggered to his bed. He took off his green coat, but was too exhausted to change into pyjamas. He fell asleep almost instantly.

When he opened his eyes again, the night had passed and the cell was filled with early morning light. He sat up and rubbed at his eyes, the fragment of a dream still stuck inside his head.

There was something in my dream, he thought.

'Bazookas,' he murmured.

It sounded like Mr Doyle and Scarlet were already up and about.

Jack stumbled down to Mr Doyle's room to find Scarlet regaling him with an account of one of the Brinkie Buckeridge books.

'—so the murder was committed with an icicle!' Scarlet was saying. 'Have you ever heard of such a thing?'

'What an original idea,' Mr Doyle murmured. 'Ah, Jack. You're finally up.'

'The engraving back at Star Beach wasn't just of any bird,' Jack told them. 'It was a heron.'

Mr Doyle frowned. 'A heron,' he said. 'I believe you're right. We're meeting Hiro for breakfast. We'll see if he has anything to add.'

Half an hour later, while eating spinach salad and miso soup, they told Hiro of Jack's revelation.

Hiro's eyes lit up. 'A heron,' he said. 'Himeji Castle is white and often called White Heron Castle, because it has been likened to a bird taking flight.'

'We will go there this morning,' Mr Doyle said.

After breakfast they were heading for their dragon-fly when they met with Dr Einstein.

'Ignatius,' he said. 'You're not leaving, are you?'

'We were planning on heading out.'

'Please be careful. There are probably still Metal-ists about who would like nothing more than to cause harm to the guest of honour.'

Mr Doyle promised he would watch his step.

Climbing aboard the dragonfly, they were soon high over Tokyo. The weather had turned sultry and it looked like another storm was on the way.

'We often have typhoons at this time of the year,' Hiro said. 'We're lucky one hasn't arrived yet.'

'Is a typhoon a type of storm?' Jack asked.

'It is a tropical cyclone. Sometimes the winds are very powerful, hundreds of miles per hour at times.' Hiro adjusted the steering of the dragonfly. 'They used to do enormous damage, but Tokyo is well equipped to deal with them these days.'

Over the next few hours, Mr Doyle stared out the window, deep in thought. At one point, he mentioned to them that a dragonfly seemed to be trailing them, but he lost sight of it. Finally, Hiro leant forward, pointing.

'There's the castle,' he said.

Jack peered down to see a squarish hill crowded with white buildings, and cherry and maple trees, surrounded by a moat.

'I didn't know Japan had any castles,' he said. 'I thought they were only in Europe.'

'Japan has a long, feudal history,' Hiro explained. 'An emperor controlled Japan until the twelfth century. Then a series of battles broke out, resulting in Japan being divided into smaller territories. Feudal lords controlled each territory with peasants providing manpower for their land and armies.'

'Europe operated in the same fashion for centuries,' Mr Doyle remarked.

Hiro brought the dragonfly down into an empty car park. The castle was made up of a main tower and three smaller ones, all white in colour with steeply pitched grey roofs. The main tower appeared to be a lookout.

It had once been a grand old building, but was now derelict and abandoned.

'That's fortunate for us,' Mr Doyle said. 'It means we can take a look around without being disturbed.'

Crossing to a gate, Mr Doyle quickly had it open with the aid of his lock pick. Ahead lay a courtyard, surrounded by cherry blossoms devoid of flowers.

'Now we need to work out the next part of the puzzle,' Mr Doyle said. 'We have a circle and the Japanese character for inside.'

'Inside could mean anything,' Scarlet said.

'What about the circle?' Jack asked, gazing about. 'Everything here looks square.'

Mr Doyle sighed. 'I suggest we begin a systematic—'

He got no further as a shot rang out, ricocheting off the wall near to Jack's ear.

CHAPTER FIFTEEN

'Run!' Mr Doyle yelled.

Jack grabbed Scarlet's hand and they raced across the courtyard to a nearby doorway. Glancing back, he saw a group of men in grey trench coats break from thick shrubs.

Mr Doyle was right, Jack realised. They were being followed.

Mr Doyle and Hiro had disappeared through a doorway on the other side of the courtyard.

We should have stayed together, Jack thought.

But it was too late now. The square paving stones deadened their footsteps as Jack and Scarlet ran down an adjacent corridor. More shots rang out in the distance and Jack heard the distinctive blast of Mr Doyle's gun, Clarabelle.

'Do you think Mr Doyle will be all right?' Scarlet asked.

'He's a resourceful man.'

They weaved through the castle, all the while hearing men shouting in German. Finally, Jack dragged Scarlet into an enclosure as a Nazi cautiously passed by, a gun in hand.

Jack sprang up behind him. 'Looking for us?' he asked, and decked him with a haymaker punch. He handed the soldier's gun to Scarlet. 'Hold onto this,' he said. 'Just in case.'

They soon reached an outer empty courtyard. Nobody had followed. In the middle of the courtyard was a low brick enclosure. Jack hurried over and saw it contained a deep well.

'This is no time for sightseeing,' Scarlet said.

'Actually, I'm having an idea. You remember the second part of the puzzle?'

'The circle?'

'What if it's a well?'

Scarlet peered down. 'It could be, I suppose,' she said.

'And the third part of the puzzle would fit, too.'

'The Japanese character for *inside*?' Scarlet stared into the hole. 'But how would anyone get down?'

Jack peered at the stonework. 'I can do it,' he said.

'You can also fall and break every bone in your body.'

'No,' he said. 'I'm sure I can get down. I just need to be careful.'

'And what will I do up here? Learn flower arranging?'

'You've got the gun. Take cover and wait.'

'My goodness,' Scarlet said, her eyes angling to a plaque attached to the wall. 'This is called Okiku's Well. Apparently she was a servant girl who worked at the castle. After losing a plate, she was thrown down the well in a fit of rage by her employer. Her ghost is said to haunt the well, as she endlessly counts plates, trying to find the missing one.'

'Did you really need to tell me that?'

'Mr Doyle doesn't believe in ghosts.'

'He's not the one climbing down the well.'

Jack carefully started down feet-first, gripping the stonework with his hands. Fortunately, there were gaps between the stones wide enough for his fingertips. The well was centuries old, but the mortar was solid, and the stones dry.

Jack controlled his breathing: from his years at the circus, he knew confidence was the most powerful ally he could have. A piece of stone broke loose, clattered into the darkness and splashed into the water.

He peered up at the opening, but saw only a perfect circle of sky. Scarlet was gone.

Good. She must be hiding.

The well seemed to go forever. *How deep is this thing?*

Jack paused. His arms were getting tired. What had seemed like a great idea at the top now seemed incredibly stupid. They could have returned later with rope. Mr Doyle was always telling him not to be so foolhardy.

Glancing up, Jack suddenly saw the silhouettes of two men. He was so terrified he almost let go of the wall. Then he realised they couldn't see him. This far down, the well was bathed in gloom.

Jack remained frozen as they chatted in German. *They must have heard a sound from the well and decided to investigate.*

Eventually the two men disappeared, but by that time Jack felt like his arms were ready to fall off. Taking a deep breath, he continued down. Another pebble dislodged and fell into the water, but this time the tiny splash was closer. Jack could now see the inky black water about ten feet below.

There's nothing here that looks like a map, he thought.

He cursed himself. His arms were aching with exertion, and a headache was building at the back of his skull. Then his eyes focused on one of the stones. The blocks around it were dark, almost black. This one was crimson and stuck out several inches from the wall.

That must be it, Jack thought. *It's that or nothing.*

He tried pulling the brick out, but nothing happened, so he tried pushing it. Suddenly a loud grinding reverberated around the well. Jack held on grimly as the section he'd clung to swivelled on an axis, exposing a small tunnel.

He climbed inside. It was so low he had to crouch. Taking a candle from his coat, he started down, remembering the story Scarlet had told him.

Her ghost is said to haunt the well...

Jack peered into the dark. *Ghosts aren't real*, he told himself.

And then a hand touched the back of his neck.

Almost screaming, he jumped, slamming his head hard against the ceiling. Swinging about in alarm, he didn't see a ghostly hand, but only a root that had grown through the brickwork.

Grimacing, Jack rubbed his head. *That'll leave a lump.* Then he spotted the small stone altar at the end of the tunnel.

He crept closer. On it sat a painted parchment, but more chilling was what sat on the parchment: a broken plate, skull and other bones that glistened in the pale candlelight. Jack swallowed. His heart was racing a mile a minute now. He didn't know a lot about anatomy, but he could tell the skull had been fractured.

Jack felt like a grave robber. Someone had died here and this was clearly an offering. Saying a small prayer, he carefully eased the parchment out and examined it.

This time the images were that of a section of coast, a ship and a rectangular box. Even Jack could see the section of coast was Japan.

This is the clearest clue yet, he thought. *But the*

Japanese coastline is thousands of miles long. And how will we get to the bottom of the sea?

Pocketing the parchment, Jack crept back to the well. There was no sign of movement at the top. This time, he was dripping with sweat, and breathing hard, as he climbed to the top.

Evening had arrived: the sky had turned indigo as the first stars appeared. Peering over the wall, Jack saw the courtyard before him was deserted.

'I advise you to climb from the well,' came a thick German voice from behind. 'Otherwise your end will be all the more painful.'

Turning his head, Jack saw Mr Doyle and Scarlet on their knees with half-a-dozen Nazis pointing guns at them.

Anton Drexler smiled as he leant close to Jack. 'Thank you, my boy,' he said. 'You have done our work for us.'

CHAPTER SIXTEEN

Jack wanted to punch Drexler in the face, but resisted the urge. Instead, he heaved himself from the well and crumpled onto the ground.

Drexler bent over and snatched the parchment from his coat. 'A cryptic clue,' he said. 'What does it mean?'

'I don't know.'

The Nazi strode over to Mr Doyle. 'And you?' he demanded. 'What is the meaning of this picture?'

'Like my assistant,' Mr Doyle said, 'I don't know. And I wouldn't tell you even if I did.'

Drexler slapped the detective across the face. Jack sprang to his feet, but one of Drexler's henchmen jabbed him with a rifle, driving him to the ground.

'It is of no matter,' Drexler said. 'We will solve it. The Kusanagi sword has waited this long. It can wait a little longer.'

'The police will be here soon,' Mr Doyle said. 'One of our friends escaped. No doubt the authorities are almost here.'

'Then it is best that I dispose of you now,' Drexler said, pulling out a revolver.

His finger tightened on the trigger. Then a single shot rang out and his weapon flew away. Gripping his bleeding hand, he ducked and ran as a hail of bullets slammed into the surrounding Germans.

Jack and the others threw themselves to the ground until the attack finished and the remaining Nazis had run away.

'Who—?' Scarlet began.

A door eased open on the opposite side of the courtyard and a Japanese man in a black suit appeared. He had steel grey hair and a tiny goatee beard.

Approaching them with an unpleasant smile, he scooped up the parchment.

'I am pleased to see the Nazis did not take the map.' He glanced at it. 'It may take some time to recover the sword, but it will eventually be mine.'

'It seems we have you to thank for our lives,' Mr Doyle said.

'One of my employees did the killing,' the man said, indicating a nearby tree. 'I have allowed you to live so you may be ransomed later to the British government.'

Mr Doyle's face darkened. 'Who are you?' he demanded.

'I am Kei Fujita,' he said, 'a businessman.'

'You're a Metalist!' Scarlet said.

'You may call me that,' Fujita said. 'The Darwinist League have plagued me for years with their dreams of clean energy and new technology.'

'You're responsible for the attacks on the symposium,' Mr Doyle said.

'And the kidnapping of your brother,' Fujita said, smiling at the look of surprise on Mr Doyle's face. 'Ah yes, I am holding Edgar. At first, my interest was only in the destruction of the Darwinist League, but then I learnt of his quest to find the sword.' He nodded. 'Can you imagine the sword's power? The ability to control the wind? To use its force to destroy your enemies? With this map I will find it and—'

The businessman stopped, his gaze fixed on a point behind them. They turned to see a man, holding a machine gun, staggering towards them.

'I have not told you to move!' Fujita snapped. 'Why have you—'

But as the man drew near, they realised a single metal star was protruding from his throat. Blood gushing from his wound, he fell down—dead.

Behind him, the red ninja dropped silently from a tree.

'Who are you?' Fujita demanded. 'Who are you working for?'

The red ninja's response was to hurl another throwing star. Fujita ducked and ran, firing a gun as he fled from the courtyard.

'Thank you,' Mr Doyle started. 'We would not have survived—'

But he never got to finish. The red ninja threw something to the ground and there was a burst of smoke. By the time it cleared, she was gone.

'She's incredible!' Scarlet said.

'Better than Bottie Bringabutt?'

'It's Brinkie Buckeridge—and, almost.'

'Fujita took the map,' Mr Doyle said. 'But at least we're alive.' Taking a piece of cheese from his pocket, he said, 'Although I've been in worse situations. One time, I investigated a case involving a rubber mouse, a teddy bear and a backyard volcano. It all started when—'

'Mr Doyle,' Jack interrupted. 'Perhaps we should find Hiro?'

'Of course.'

Carefully navigating through the castle, they eventually reached one of the outer gates with no sign of either Drexler or Fujita. Night had fallen by the time they reached their dragonfly.

'Mr Doyle?' came a voice from the gloom.

'Hiro?'

'Where have you been?' Hiro asked, emerging from the bushes. 'I became lost in the castle. Is everything all right?'

They all laughed. Climbing into the dragonfly's

cabin, Mr Doyle quickly related what had happened.

Hiro swallowed. 'Not only is Fujita a Metalist, but he is also one of the deadliest gang bosses in Japan,' he said. 'If he doesn't ransom Edgar to the British government, then he will kill him.'

Mr Doyle started. 'But surely the police—'

'—will do nothing,' Hiro said. 'You know they need evidence before they can arrest him.'

'What can we do?'

'Fujita has a private tower in the heart of Tokyo,' Hiro said, thoughtfully. 'Fortunately, I know the man who designed and built it.'

'You're suggesting we break in and save Edgar?'

'It is his only chance. And we should act quickly.'

As they zoomed over the darkened Japanese landscape, heading back towards Tokyo, Mr Doyle was quiet. The wind had picked up now and it was colder. Lightning flashed on the horizon.

Jack watched Mr Doyle. The detective was obviously conflicted over putting them at risk to save Edgar. What had he said about his brother?

A scoundrel...a consummate thief...broken into a dozen museums over the years...

Approaching the heart of the city, Hiro glanced back at them.

'What is your decision?' he asked.

Mr Doyle sighed. 'I must try to save Edgar,' he said. 'If I can.'

'Good.'

'But I must do it alone.'

'No,' Jack protested. 'We're coming with you.'

'You can't—'

'We are,' Scarlet interrupted. 'And you can't stop us.'

The detective sighed. 'When I took you on as my assistants,' he said, 'I imagined you would obey my orders.'

'Mr Doyle,' Jack said. 'You have not taught us to obey. You have taught us to *think*.'

Hiro grinned. 'I believe you are outnumbered,' he said.

'All right,' Mr Doyle said. '*We* will save Edgar.'

'Good,' Hiro said. 'I will take us to Sato. He is the man who designed Fujita's tower.'

He directed the dragonfly to the south of the city, down through a canyon of buildings to a narrow alley of ancient homes. After parking the dragonfly, Hiro knocked at one of the doors. A young Japanese woman answered. Hiro said a few words, and she led them into a living room.

There were no chairs. Jack and the others sat on the floor around a small table. An elderly man appeared, his face creasing with anger as Hiro spoke to him in Japanese.

'You are Doyle?' the old man said, finally turning to the detective.

'I am.'

'Helping you could cost me my life. Why should I assist you?'

Mr Doyle swallowed. 'The future peace of the world is at stake,' he said. 'Including the lives of millions of people. Not to mention my scoundrel of a brother.'

Sato nodded grimly. 'Family is both a blessing and curse,' he said.

He left, only to return a few minutes later with old plans of a one-hundred storey tower. He laid them across the table and they crowded around. Jack couldn't see any way they could break in.

Sato pointed at the ninety-ninth level. 'When I designed the tower,' he said, 'Fujita told me to put cells here, beneath his penthouse. He said he liked to keep his enemies close.'

'This is impossible,' Jack said. 'There's no way we can fight our way up all those levels.'

'That will not be necessary,' Hiro said, his face lighting up. 'I think we should go straight to the top.'

CHAPTER SEVENTEEN

Hiro struggled to control the dragonfly as they flew across Tokyo. Rain poured into the cabin through the open doors. The cloud cover was thick with visibility limited to one hundred feet.

We'll be lucky if we don't crash into the tower, Jack thought.

'We're almost there,' Hiro said.

'Are you sure?' Jack asked.

A huge shape loomed in front of them, and Hiro swung the vessel to narrowly miss the tower. 'I'm certain,' he said.

Fujita's building was a circular shaft, made from iron and glass. The penthouse was half dome and half rooftop garden. The teardrop-shaped landing pad hung off the side, pointing south. Lights were on inside, but whoever was home wouldn't be able to see the dragonfly through the mist and rain.

Mr Doyle took Jack's arm. 'My boy,' he said. 'I can go first, if you wish.'

Jack smiled. 'But I have a better chance of succeeding.'

Even Scarlet looked worried. 'Jack,' she said. 'In case things go wrong...in case this doesn't work...' Staring into his eyes, she leant forward and planted a kiss on his lips. 'Be careful.'

At any other time, Jack's head would have exploded with excitement, but now he simply nodded. One wrong slip and...no more Jack Mason.

Hiro descended to the ninety-eighth level and rounded the building to a section marked on the map as *Storage*. Fighting to keep the dragonfly twenty feet from the tower, Hiro nodded to Mr Doyle.

The detective lifted an oversized gun from the floor as Scarlet indicated a darkened window.

'That's it!' she yelled.

Mr Doyle leant out the window. 'Keep us steady!'

He fired the gun. A metal arrow with a rope attached flew across the gap and smashed through the window. It stuck fast to a wall inside the room. As the detective secured the rope to the dragonfly, Jack attached a safety clip from his belt to the line.

Jack eased himself from the cabin and started dragging himself across the gap. He tried not to think about the mile separating him from the ground. If he released the rope, the safety clip would save him, but nothing could be done if Hiro lost control of the dragonfly or the arrow pulled loose.

Hauling himself across the gap, Jack finally climbed into the storage room. Out of the howling gale, the tower's interior was strangely quiet. He checked the arrow. They were lucky. It had impaled itself firmly into a wall. It would not break free.

After signalling to the others, Jack watched Mr Doyle and Scarlet cross then helped them into the room.

'My goodness,' Scarlet said, breathless. 'Brinkie would be proud.'

'I'm sure she would,' Jack said.

Hiro had to keep the dragonfly stationary while they searched for Edgar Doyle. Jack didn't envy him his task.

Mr Doyle eased open the door. Beyond lay a corridor with a barrel roof, lit only by tiny gas lights. Wordlessly, they followed it to the end. There were fire stairs, but according to Sato, these were alarmed. Jack, Scarlet and Mr Doyle forced the elevator doors open, revealing a shaft stretching all the way to the bottom.

'Don't fall,' Scarlet advised.

'Great advice,' Jack said. 'I'll be sure to follow it.'

The building groaned.

'That's nothing to worry about,' Mr Doyle assured them. 'These towers are made to move with the wind.'

Jack nodded, peering up the shaft. Crossbars reinforced the walls.

He gripped one and stepped over to it, his heart palpitating. One wrong move and it would be a very quick journey to the bottom.

He climbed up to the next level, disengaged the mechanism controlling the elevator doors and carefully pulled it open.

The corridor beyond was empty. The cells lining it on both sides were also empty. If Edgar was here, he was around the other side. There were no guards. After all, who in their right mind would try to break in through the side of the building?

Jack stuck his head over the edge. 'Throw me the rope,' he whispered.

Within seconds, Mr Doyle and Scarlet were beside him.

'My boy,' Mr Doyle said, 'you've done exceedingly well.'

'We're not out of this yet.'

They hurried down the corridor, but Edgar was nowhere to be seen. Jack was just about to give up when they reached a cell with a man curled up on a bunk, reading a book.

'Piggie?' he exclaimed.

Piggie?

Jack and Scarlet looked at each other.

'Don't call me that,' Mr Doyle snapped. 'We're here to help you escape.'

'A shame,' Edgar Doyle said. 'I was catching up on my reading.'

Mr Doyle had the cell open in seconds. Now Jack had an opportunity to look more closely at Mr Doyle's brother. He was dressed as if he'd stepped straight out of a renaissance painting. Taller than his brother, and thinner, with a long, thin moustache that twirled up at the ends, he wore a cavalier hat, adorned with red and blue feathers. It matched his voluminous blue pants and crimson shirt. The thick black belt encircling his waist appeared to be made from the same material as his boots—alligator skin.

Edgar took a deep breath of air as he stepped free, slapping his chest.

'*Now go we in content. To liberty,*' he said, '*and not to banishment.*'

'Pardon?' Jack said.

'From the Bard,' Edgar said. 'William Shakespeare's *As You Like It.*'

'Edgar has always loved Shakespeare,' Mr Doyle explained drily, introducing Jack and Scarlet.

'You've adopted children, Piggie!' Edgar said. 'Good for you!'

'They're my assistants,' Mr Doyle said. 'And don't call me Piggie. My name is Ignatius. And what is that terrible smell?'

Edgar looked insulted. 'You never did have much in the way of style,' he said. 'It's *Mon Paris*. One of the world's most expensive colognes. You know I've always loved good cologne.'

'As long as you didn't have to pay for it.'

'*Tsk, tsk*. That's all in the past. Now you must tell me what has happened.'

He listened as they gave him a potted version of their adventures.

'I see,' Edgar said. 'I am pleased to hear you continued searching for the sword. I was apprehended by Fujita as I returned from Daikonshima.'

'At least we've found you. Now we need to escape.'

'After retrieving the parchment,' Edgar said. 'It may still contain valuable information.'

'We're doing no such thing,' Mr Doyle snapped. 'We're getting you out of here, and forgetting all about this blasted sword. It's almost gotten us killed half-a-dozen times already.'

'And leave behind the most important artefact in human history? What's wrong with you, Piggie?'

Jack stepped forward. 'We've got to go,' he said. 'Fujita might turn up at any moment.'

'All the more reason for us to stay. We can take the map from him and—'

Mr Doyle grabbed Edgar's lapel. 'Listen to me,' he said, quietly. 'You can either come with us, or stay. Which is it?'

Edgar gently shook free. 'Why,' he said, 'I'm coming with you. Who needs the most powerful weapon in human history when you can enjoy tea and scones before a raging fire?' As they headed down the corridor, he continued to Jack and Scarlet. 'I assume my brother has told you about my adventures.'

'Er,' Jack said. 'He said you used to be a thief.'

'Thief is such a strong word,' Edgar said. 'I tend to think of myself as a borrower. A lover of paintings, sculptures, jewellery—'

'But didn't they belong to other people?'

'I like to borrow them for long periods,' Edgar said, flashing a cheerful smile. 'And I ask you: who really owns anything? Life is so fleeting. One must seize opportunities as they arise.'

Mr Doyle led them back to the elevator. Jack was pleased to see the rope was still attached. All they had to do was—

He stopped. A sound was coming from the elevator shaft. Jack peered down to see a rising elevator.

Bazookas.

Someone was coming.

CHAPTER EIGHTEEN

'Maybe we can use another elevator,' Jack suggested. 'Or the stairs.'

'Don't you remember?' Scarlet said. 'There isn't another elevator. Fujita only has one. And the alarm will go off if we use the stairs.'

'This really isn't a problem,' Mr Doyle said. 'The elevator will pass, probably severing the rope. But we have another piece. We'll simply wait here until he passes.'

'A most agreeable idea, Piggie,' Edgar said. 'And it will give me a chance to straighten my cravat.'

'Why are you dressed like that?' Jack asked.

'A man must always look his best. As the Bard said, *All the world's a stage, and all—*'

'What Edgar is really saying,' Mr Doyle interrupted, 'is that he loves to be in the limelight.'

'Not at all!' Edgar protested, spraying on more perfume. 'Any light will do.'

Standing at the edge of the shaft, Jack watched the elevator climb higher and higher. It slowed as it approached its final destination—the floor above.

'Best stand back,' Mr Doyle said.

'Of course,' Edgar said, dragging Jack to him. 'You stand back while Jack and I retrieve the map.'

Edgar hauled Jack through the open gap and towards the approaching elevator. Smashing through the ceiling hatch, they landed on the man inside—Fujita.

It had all happened so quickly that Jack couldn't speak at first.

'What—? Why—?' he spluttered at Edgar as he staggered back from the unconscious crime boss. 'Why did you do that?'

'Because we can't let the Kusanagi sword fall into the wrong hands,' Edgar explained patiently, searching Fujita's pockets. 'And he was exceptionally nasty to me. I asked him repeatedly for my favourite blend of *Russian caravan* tea and he would not supply it.'

'But...but...'

'You sound like a steam engine, Jack. Tell me what's on your mind.'

'Mr Doyle says the sword isn't real.'

'The sword *is* real,' Edgar said, pulling out the parchment. 'Ah, here we are.'

As the doors slid open to the Penthouse, Edgar pressed the button for the floor below, but he was already too late. Two security guards stood opposite. Their mouths dropped open at the sight of Jack, Edgar and the unconscious Fujita.

'Two vodka martinis,' Edgar instructed. 'Hold the ice.'

The doors slid shut before the men could react.

'Mr Doyle!' Jack said. 'I mean...'

'Call me Edgar.'

'Those men will come after us!'

An alarm broke out as the elevator descended.

'Then we'd best hurry,' Edgar said. 'Have a way out, do you?'

Jack explained about the dragonfly as the elevator reached the level below. The doors opened to reveal a furious Mr Doyle and Scarlet.

'Are you insane?' Mr Doyle yelled at his brother.

'Not at all, Piggie,' Edgar said. 'I knew retrieving the map would only take a moment. Now let's get out of here.'

Ten minutes later they were back in the dragonfly.

'Edgar-san!' Hiro yelled. 'It is good to see you again!'

'And you, Hiro,' Edgar replied, slapping him on the back. 'How is your aunt's miso soup?'

'Save the reminiscing for later,' Mr Doyle said, cutting them free from the tower. 'We must hurry.'

Hiro urged the dragonfly into the storm.

'You see,' Edgar said to them. 'I knew we'd be fine.

I propose a celebratory dinner. Possibly some duck, a vegetable terrine followed by—'

Bang!

Something slammed into the rear of the dragonfly.

'They're firing at us!' Hiro yelled. 'We're hit.'

Jack glanced back through the rear window as Hiro increased the dragonfly's speed. Two other dragonflies, small cannons fitted their heads, were in pursuit. There was a flash and another projectile slammed into them.

Hiro drove the damaged beast on through the storm. They lost one of their pursuers almost immediately, but the other remained on their tail, firing again.

Hiro pulled back the wheel and they went into a sharp ascent. He braked, allowing their pursuer to fly under them, then crashed their dragonfly down onto them. The other dragonfly flipped over and spun away into the torrential storm.

'We've got to land!' he yelled. 'Our dragonfly's not going to survive.'

They were hurtling towards the ground. Jack caught a glimpse of a rapidly approaching dark forest. At the last possible moment, Hiro pulled back on the wheel and the dragonfly levelled out, scraping across the tops of trees. Then the creature gave a hideous shriek as a wing slammed into something.

They slewed sideways and everyone was thrown against a wall. Jack felt his stomach heave.

This is it, he thought. *The end.*

But Hiro somehow regained control, aiming towards

a small plain in the forest. The dragonfly swung about, the bottom hitting the ground, before skidding for what seemed forever.

Finally, they stopped. The wind shrieked outside and rain poured.

Untangling themselves, Jack climbed from the cabin and staggered into the downpour.

Scarlet gave a cry. 'Hiro!' she said. 'Is he all right?'

Hiro was either unconscious or dead. Carefully easing him from the wreckage, Mr Doyle checked for injuries.

'Mr Doyle?' Jack called.

'Just a nasty knock on the head,' Mr Doyle said.

Edgar led Jack and Scarlet to the middle of the clearing. Raising his arms to the sky, he said, '*I am resolved to bear a greater storm than any thou canst conjure up to-day.*' Turning to Jack, he added, '*King Henry VI, Part Two.*'

'How do you remember all these quotes?' Jack asked.

'There is a simple answer,' Edgar said. 'I have a superior intellect.'

'But you are completely without modesty,' Scarlet said.

'Modesty is a word for dishonesty. Best to focus on the truth.'

'But as a thief—'

'Ah,' Edgar cut her off. '*But, soft! what light through yonder window breaks?* If I'm not mistaken, that's a house beyond those trees.'

A groan came from behind. They saw Mr Doyle helping Hiro to his feet.

'How are you feeling?' Jack asked.

'My head hurts,' Hiro said. 'But I am otherwise fine.'

'That was magnificent flying,' Scarlet said.

'We would have died if not for your skills,' Mr Doyle said.

Even in the pale light, Jack could see Hiro reddening.

'I did my best,' he said. 'But the dragonfly is dead. Now we must find our way to town.'

'Right-o!' Edgar declared. 'First we need food and shelter. Then we have a sword to find.'

Jack saw Mr Doyle roll his eyes.

They traipsed through the forest to the house where Edgar asked for directions. It seemed they were still several miles from Tokyo, but a train was due at the local station soon.

It was almost midnight by the time they stumbled into the old Tokyo jail. Einstein was just leaving the dining hall.

'Good Lord!' he said. 'What on earth happened to you?'

After introducing Edgar, Mr Doyle made up the story that their dragonfly had collided with another vehicle and crashed.

'I'm glad you're safe,' Einstein said. 'There's a meeting being held tomorrow to discuss the rest of the symposium. The Japanese government is concerned for the safety of the delegates and has arranged for us to be moved to another venue. They say it will be safer for all concerned.'

'Surely it would be better if the symposium were cancelled?'

'The Hot Earth Accord must be signed,' Einstein said, gravely. 'It might take years to get both scientists and diplomats to such an event again. By then it would be too late for the planet—and for mankind.'

'Then I look forward to hearing more tomorrow,' Mr Doyle said, forcing a smile. 'We'll see you in the morning.'

Hiro thanked them and said he would return then. Jack and the others ate a small meal in the dining room before trudging back to their rooms where Mr Doyle pointed out a cell for his brother.

Edgar rubbed his hands together. 'It's just like the old days, Piggie,' he said.

Mr Doyle stared at him. 'If showing a complete disregard for everyone around you is what you mean,' he said, 'then you're absolutely right.'

Edgar slapped him on the arm. 'Don't be like that,' he said. 'We're the Doyle brothers! Together after all these years.'

'The prime minister asked me to find you. I have. Now, the sooner I see the back of you, the better.'

Without saying another word, Mr Doyle turned and retreated to his room.

CHAPTER NINETEEN

'Thank you for your patience,' Dr Einstein said.

Almost a hundred people had gathered in the jail's dining room. Looking about, Jack saw scientists, diplomats, security staff and journalists. Mr Doyle and the others were at his side. The detective had barely acknowledged Edgar that morning, simply grunting a greeting as they headed off to the meeting.

'I have an announcement to make that I think will make many of us very excited,' Einstein continued. 'We are moving to Mizu City.'

'Mizu,' Jack murmured. 'That's the—'

'—underwater city,' Scarlet said, her eyes wide. 'Bazookas.'

'A single airship will be transporting us there,' Einstein continued. 'Please have your bags ready. We will be assembling on the roof.'

In the excited buzz that broke out among the crowd, Jack noticed that Mr Doyle did not look pleased.

'I would prefer we returned to London,' he said.

'But the prime minister ordered you to find Edgar and the sword,' Jack said.

'Edgar has been found, but I have doubts that the Kusanagi sword will ever be retrieved. It could take months, or years, to find it—assuming the sea has not already reduced it to rust.'

They returned to their rooms and packed their few belongings. Hiro was unable to join them as he was needed at home. Edgar went out to buy a few changes of clothing and some toiletries. On his return, Jack ran into him in the corridor, looking pleased with himself.

'So we're travelling to Mizu City,' Edgar said, stroking his moustache. 'Wonderful!'

'Have you wanted to go there?'

'Jack,' Edgar laughed. 'Did you not see the map?' He pulled the parchment from his pocket. 'The sword is clearly somewhere in the vicinity of the underwater city.'

Jack stared. The 'X' marking the spot could have been anywhere within a hundred mile radius of the city.

'That's a big area to search,' he said. 'And how did it end up there?'

'One of the ancient legends surrounding the Kusanagi sword describes it being lost in a shipwreck.'

'But that was centuries ago.'

'We mustn't give up,' Edgar said. 'The British government is depending on us. Besides,' he added, 'it's a powerful weapon. We mustn't allow it to fall into enemy hands.'

'Mr Doyle, er, your brother, says that it's just a legend.'

'A tapestry was recovered last year in northern Japan illustrating a battle where the sword was used. Historical figures from that period are also present, meaning the sword *must* have existed.'

The old man in the garden said it was real, Jack thought. *Now Edgar is saying the same thing.*

Mr Doyle stuck his head through the doorway. 'We're ready to leave,' he said, frowning at Edgar. 'What are you doing?'

'I'm coming with you,' Edgar said. 'I wouldn't miss your closing address for all the world.'

Now Mr Doyle peered more closely at the two of them.

'I hope you're not filling Jack's head with foolishness,' he said.

'Wouldn't dream of it. *The fool doth think he is wise, but the wise man knows himself to be a fool,*' Edgar said.

After Mr Doyle left, Edgar leant in close to Jack. 'Let's just keep this between ourselves,' he said. 'Mum's the word.'

'I don't want to lie to Mr Doyle.'

'And I would never ask you to,' Edgar said. 'But all truth is relative. I once borrowed a painting from a French art gallery that had been borrowed six times before.'

'You mean stolen?' Jack said.

'Such a crass word! But who was the real owner?' He gave his moustache a twirl. 'Finders keepers, that's what I say.'

Jack nodded, unsure.

They headed up to the roof where Scarlet, Mr Doyle and most of the members of the symposium had already assembled. The storm the night before had left the sky over Tokyo clear, but the air sultry, with another bank of clouds crowding the horizon.

Scarlet sidled over, staring at Edgar. 'Where did you get those clothes?' she asked.

Jack glanced at Edgar Doyle. His cavalier hat was the same, but he was wearing a brand new pair of leather pants and white shirt.

'I went out shopping,' Edgar said. 'A man must look his best.'

'You didn't steal them?' Scarlet said. 'I'm sure they were in the window of that department store over the road, and I saw the police—'

'As if I'd do something like that!' Edgar laughed. He pointed over her shoulder. 'My goodness! Look at that!'

He was pointing at an airship that had just appeared from behind some buildings.

'Bazookas,' Jack said. 'It's a...a...'

'A flower,' Scarlet said, astonished.

'It is,' Einstein said, joining them. 'Although some fairly dramatic modifications have been made.'

The crimson ship was shaped like a trumpet flower. A hundred-feet long and twenty wide, the front curled back, revealing the bridge.

'That's not glass,' Einstein explained, pointing to the windows. 'It's derived from gossamer—spider thread. The ship uses photosynthesis to create energy. Heated air is fired from the rear. It's the first of its kind.'

Livanov pushed through the crowd to them. 'Impressed by our little surprise?' she asked. 'We've christened her the *Carlton*, after her designer.'

What a time to be alive, Jack thought. *Dragonflies and flowers for ships, whales for submarines.*

At the same time, he felt a shiver of fear. The familiar world he had always known was dying and a new one taking its place.

What is next?

Minutes later, they were aboard and Jack was seated with the others on the strangest bench he had ever seen. Hard as mahogany, it was one of twenty rows that grew straight out of the floor. A horn blared, bowlines made from some kind of vine were cast off and the *Carlton* moved away.

The strangest thing about this ship is the silence.

Jack had spent his whole life around steam. Its production meant there was always the crackling of fire, chugging engines and the banging of metal. This vessel moved in almost total silence, the only sound being an odd wheezing from beneath.

'Those are the ship's bellows,' Einstein explained.

'You said the ship was powered by photosynthesis?' Scarlet said. 'That's sunlight, isn't it?'

'It is, and you're probably wondering how the ship works when there's no sunlight?'

'I am.'

'The excess energy is stored in bladders that run along the bottom. They're still rudimentary, and only hold about four hours of charge, but we're working to improve them.'

Tokyo passed beneath them as Einstein continued to speak, but Jack's focus was on the city.

This is a city of the future, he thought. *The whole world will be like this one day.*

It was all very strange. He'd always thought of London as being the centre of civilisation, but now he realised it was just another cog in a very big machine.

But what about the Kusanagi sword? Where did it fit in, a mythical sword with magical powers? Mr Doyle had scoffed at it, but Edgar thought it was real.

Is there room in the world for both science and magic?

They soon headed east over open sea. It was late morning and the sea was busy with fleets of fishing boats. Peering down at them, Jack could imagine a time when they became obsolete.

You'll probably be driving sharks in a few years.

When the ship had left Japan and the fishing boats behind, Jack and Scarlet went to the rear where it was quieter.

'Edgar says the Kusanagi sword is real,' Jack said, staring at the sea. 'We can't leave without finding it.'

'Don't be silly, Jack. Mr Doyle's found his brother. We should return to England.'

'But the prime minister ordered us to find it. Otherwise, the sword may fall into Fujita's hands, or Drexler.'

'You heard Mr Doyle. There probably isn't any sword, and if there is, it doesn't have mystical powers.'

'Maybe science isn't the answer to everything.'

Suddenly a cry came from within the ship. Jack and Scarlet ran inside to find people pressed to the portside windows. Floating in the ocean was a wooden warehouse on a square metal barge.

Jack frowned. 'That's not quite what I was expecting,' he said.

Einstein sidled up. 'That's Mizu Dock,' he explained. 'A diving bell drops from it to the city.'

The airship swung in low over the platform. Lines were lowered and minutes later Jack disembarked onto the swaying dock. He peered at the distant horizon. They were in the middle of nowhere. It was hard to believe one of the wonders of the modern age lay beneath.

The crowd shuffled into the warehouse to find an iron ball suspended by a pulley over a pool.

'That must be the diving bell,' Scarlet said.

Warehouse staff directed Jack and the others up

metal stairs to the bell's entrance. A spiral staircase led to three floors below. There was no seating inside, but oxygen tanks lined the walls in case of emergency. As the hatch closed, and the diving bell was gently lowered into the water, Livanov approached Jack and Scarlet.

'Are you excited?' she asked.

'Absolutely,' Jack said. 'How long will it take to reach the city?'

'Hours. People can become seriously ill if they descend too quickly.'

'Is that the bends?' Scarlet asked.

'It is,' Dr Livanov said, delighted. 'It's lovely to see a young woman interested in science.' She went on to explain the condition was caused by nitrogen leaving the cells too quickly. 'It can cause extreme pain in the joints, even death.'

As they chatted, Jack noticed Mr Doyle standing by himself, peering out at the water. Jack excused himself to join him.

'You seem quiet, sir,' Jack said as they began their descent. 'Deep in thought?'

'Just thinking about Edgar,' Mr Doyle said. 'It's rather a shock seeing him after all this time.'

'You've never missed him?'

'I've never *forgiven* him.' Mr Doyle sighed. 'My father and stepmother died a few years after Edgar was first sent to prison. I believe it broke their hearts, and contributed to their early deaths.'

'Do you mind if I ask you a question, sir? A personal one?'

'Please do.'

'Well,' Jack said, 'Edgar has that name for you. Piggie...'

Mr Doyle sighed. 'I was a little rotund as a child,' he said. 'By the time I was a young man, I had shed all my excess weight, but Edgar has teased me about it ever since.'

Outside, the water had turned pitch black. Then finally someone gave a cry from one of the portholes.

'There it is! I can see it.'

Mr Doyle and Jack crowded around a window.

'Bazookas,' Jack muttered.

Mizu City looked like a glowing strand of pearls on the ocean bottom. Everything around was in complete darkness. The enormous spheres were a mile in circumference, translucent green, and linked by a single iron tunnel. The upper half of each sphere was transparent. They contained apartment blocks, warehouses, factories and roads.

'I wonder what goes on there,' Scarlet said, pointing at the darkened bottom of the spheres.

'I read about it in a book,' Jack said. 'That's where they keep all the pipes, air-conditioning and maintenance systems.'

Einstein's voice came over the speaking tube. 'Despite their shape, we refer to each of the chambers as domes. Domes One, Two, Three and Four are living and research quarters. Five is used for energy production and waste management.'

'Truly incredible,' Mr Doyle said. 'It looks like a living thing.'

Dr Livanov, hearing his comment, stepped over. 'It *is* a living thing,' she said. 'The city was grown from a modified form of sargassum seaweed.'

'And inside?'

'The buildings are made from a coral variant, but the power supply is still steam, unfortunately,' she said. 'The biggest holdup during construction was the transportation of the steam-powered generators and factories to the domes.'

The diving bell continued to descend. A few minutes later it dropped down through a hole in Dome One.

Looking up through the porthole, Jack saw the top contract tight. Then the water drained from the chamber, revealing a walkway leading to a hatch at the bottom.

They left the diving bell one by one and entered a cylindrical, metal room with a ramp running along it. Great iron hatches were at each end. One opened and they all walked through. A moment later they stepped into the dome.

Jack stared about in wonder. It was a cityscape, not unlike London, with buildings, parks and roads. A library and town hall were directly in front. Further down the street were shopfronts, but only a few businesses were open. A single steamcar trundled down one of the roads.

The place smelt like the sea. The light leaked beyond

the transparent walls, and Jack saw a school of fish zoom by, followed by a squid.

Jack swallowed. It was frightening to think that the walls were the only thing saving them from being crushed by the pressure.

'Don't be too alarmed,' Einstein said, seeing the worried expression on his face. 'The walls are stronger than steel.'

'And if something were to break through?'

Einstein hesitated. 'That would be worrisome,' he said. 'But not even a whale could do that.'

Reporters and photographers were quick to set up bellows cameras and take pictures, using flash lamps. As the guest of honour, Mr Doyle was asked to pose with scientists. After Scarlet had wandered off to look into one of the shops, Edgar sidled up to Jack.

'Incredible, isn't it?' Edgar said.

'It's amazing,' Jack said. 'I never knew the city was being...grown.'

'And more than that,' Edgar said, quietly. 'We're closer than ever to the Kusanagi sword. It may only lie a few miles from here.'

'So how—'

'—will we get to it?' Edgar said. 'There is a plan in the works, my boy. I'll keep you advised.' He reached into his pocket and sprayed on some more cologne. 'Ah, nothing like *Soir de Lyon*!'

'Is that a different fragrance?'

'It is! A man must reinvent himself to confuse his

enemies! A different appearance. A different scent—'

'But where did you get it from?'

'A lovely man in the diving bell gave it to me,' Edgar said, gripping Jack's arm. 'The generosity of strangers is profound.'

The newcomers were taken to the *Imperial* hotel in Dome Two. It was a huge stone building, more like a small palace than a hotel, with marble floors and a wide, twisting staircase. Potted palms decorated the foyer. A Japanese restaurant was to the right of the reception desk. Jack had to remind himself that they were miles under the sea.

Their rooms were comfortable chambers on the third floor. Jack, Scarlet and Mr Doyle would share a room while Edgar was across the hall. The rooms had been decorated in the Western style, and so they had beds rather than futons. Jack was rather pleased. Futons took a little getting used to.

He spent a moment unpacking his few belongings. He patted his pockets, relieved to find he still had his compass and locket of his parents.

A knock at the door turned out to be Edgar. He smiled broadly at Mr Doyle as he entered.

'Piggie!' he boomed. 'You've done very well for yourself. You've clearly got friends in high places!'

'I've been friends with Einstein for some years,' Mr Doyle said, sourly.

'I could get quite accustomed to this!'

Mr Doyle's eyes narrowed. 'Don't bother,' he said.

'We're only here for a few days so I can give a presentation, and then we're leaving.'

'So soon?' Edgar glanced sideways at Jack. 'But we're so close to finding the sword.'

'The sword may never be found,' Mr Doyle said. 'I hope you'll forget this hocus-pocus and return to England.'

'Piggie...'

'And stop calling me that blasted name!' Mr Doyle exploded. 'My name is Ignatius!'

Scarlet interrupted. 'Possibly we could go on a tour of the city?' she said. 'I noticed one was being planned in the lobby.'

'Wonderful,' Mr Doyle said, regaining his composure. 'We might as well make the most of our time while we're here.'

They returned to the lobby where most of the scientists, diplomats and journalists had already assembled. The city manager, a man by the name of Elias Blair, had offered to personally show the party around. A stout man, he had a huge handlebar moustache and a deep booming voice.

'Welcome to Mizu City!' he declared. 'Today I will show you the Eighth Wonder of the Modern World. What you'll be seeing is the future! If you have any questions, please let me know. If there is a break in the dome, everyone hold your breath!'

He laughed, but nobody else did.

After taking them through domes one to four, Blair

pointed out empty apartment blocks, government buildings and facilities. Someone finally asked him about the
population of Mizu City.

'Only a few hundred people currently live here,'
he said. 'Your group has added considerably to that
population.'

'Why so few people?' a journalist inquired.

'While the city is fully operational, many of its
systems are still being tested.'

The fifth dome was different. Filled with machinery,
it smelt of smoke and steam. Jack noticed it was hotter
too.

'Coal is shipped down here three times a week,'
Blair said. 'The main furnace connects to three boilers
that power the entire city.'

Someone asked him about a building jutting against
the outside of the sphere.

'That's the submarine dock,' he said. 'It's not
functioning—yet.'

The smell was particularly bad at the far end of
the dome. Blair pointed out a large rectangular building
adjacent to the curving wall. The sign above the door
read *Waste Management*.

'Everybody produces waste,' Blair said, 'but nobody
likes talking about it.'

He broke into deep, booming laughter, but the
audience only gave a polite smile. Undeterred, Blair
led them inside. As they strolled along an overhead
walkway, he pointed to a vast drawer as long and wide

as an Olympic swimming pool only five times deeper.

'Foods scraps and other organic waste is collected here,' he said. 'The cover locks into place, and the waste is shunted out to the open sea. Non-organic waste is either burnt or taken back to the surface.'

'And when it's dumped into the ocean?' Scarlet asked.

'It's eaten by marine life. We don't release anything toxic into the environment.'

A distant crash rang through the dome. Blair paled.

'I don't like the sound of that,' he said.

The group raced back through to Dome One. Here they found a group of engineers assembled around the chamber containing the diving bell.

'What happened?' Einstein demanded.

A man introduced himself to the group as Engineer Browne. 'There's been an explosion in the diving bell,' he said.

'What?'

'It's badly damaged.' The engineer looked around at their faces. 'Until we fix it, we're trapped down here.'

CHAPTER TWENTY

'What a wonderful accident!' Edgar announced.

Jack, Scarlet, Mr Doyle and Edgar were eating cucumber sandwiches and drinking tea in Dome One's only open café. The whole city was strangely quiet since the incident involving the diving bell. Everyone was on edge knowing they couldn't escape the city.

Mr Doyle put down his sandwich. 'Edgar,' he said. 'Are you so foolish as to believe it was an accident?'

'What are you saying, Piggie?' he asked. 'That it was deliberate?'

'You are really the most obtuse man—' Mr Doyle stopped himself. 'Fujita would love to see us dead, not to mention Drexler and his Nazi cronies. And what about the scientists gathered here?' he asked. 'The Metalists could wipe out its top scientists with one blow.' He shook his head. 'I was a fool to ever agree to come.'

'There is a bright side,' Edgar said.

'And that is?'

'It gives us time to work on finding the sword. If we—'

Mr Doyle leapt to his feet. For a moment, it looked like he might actually attack his brother, but somehow he managed to restrain himself.

'I never want to hear about that ridiculous sword again,' he seethed.

Jack spoke up. 'There must be another way out,' he said. 'What about a submarine?'

Sitting back down, Mr Doyle said, 'One could make it down here. But the dock isn't operational. For the moment, it seems we're stuck here.'

Jack sighed. Many of the scientists were working on a plan to re-establish contact with the surface while the city engineers repaired the diving bell. There was no indication how long that might take. It could be days, weeks—or even longer.

Finishing their meal, they started back to their hotel. On the way, Blair raced up to them.

'Are you Doyle?' he asked.

'Yes,' Edgar and Ignatius answered simultaneously.

'Er, there's been a murder.'

'I see,' Mr Doyle said. 'It's probably me you'll be wanting then.'

Returning to the *Imperial*, Mr Doyle told his brother to remain in the foyer. Edgar looked like he wanted to argue, but clamped his mouth when he saw the expression on Mr Doyle's face.

On the fourth floor, Jack and the others were shown into a large suite with a view overlooking the city. It was a neat and tidy chamber, and all looked completely ordinary—except for the dead man lying in the middle of the floor.

'This is Ryan Davidson,' Blair said. 'He's worked at Mizu City since the beginning.'

Mr Doyle gingerly examined the body. 'He's been dead about an hour,' he said. 'A single stab wound to the heart.'

Jack did an examination of the room, but there was little to discover. It appeared the assailant had knocked on the door and killed Davidson almost immediately.

Mr Doyle frowned as he looked around. 'Nothing was stolen,' he said, thoughtfully chewing on a piece of cheese. 'And the style of murder is coldly efficient. It's unlikely to be a crime of passion. So why would someone want this man dead?'

'And why now?' Jack wondered, aloud.

Mr Doyle stared at him. 'Of course!' he said, turning to Blair. 'What was Davidson's job?'

'He's the manager of the power plant.'

'You must take us there! Immediately!'

They raced through the city.

'What does this have to do with Davidson?' Blair

puffed, trying to keep up with Mr Doyle. 'Why was he killed?'

'Because Davidson would be able to undo whatever calamity is about to befall the power supply.'

When they arrived, they found the doors to the power plant locked.

'This is strange,' Blair said. 'These are normally open.'

They entered silently. The power plant was enormous, but most of it was automated. Coal fed into hoppers that were delivered to a furnace. Water boiled in vast chambers that turned to steam, supplying the whole city with heat, light and power.

Jack peered at the dozens of gantries running across the building. There wasn't a person to be seen.

'Is it normally this quiet?' Mr Doyle asked.

'Everything is self-maintaining,' Blair said. 'Davidson and a repair team check the systems daily.'

Entering the office overlooking the plant, Mr Doyle pointed to the main control panel. It had been smashed to pieces.

'Looks like someone's been busy,' he said.

'Good heavens!' Blair exploded.

Jack stared at the controls. 'What does this mean?' he asked.

'It means we're in serious trouble,' Blair said. 'The city needs power to extract air from the water. Without it, we'll suffocate.'

A sound came from an upper gantry. Jack turned to see a figure, clad from head to toe in a maintenance outfit, dashing away.

'Quick!' Mr Doyle yelled. 'We must catch them!'

Jack, Scarlet and Mr Doyle gave chase. The maintenance clothing had a hood, making it impossible to identify them. The person disappeared behind the main furnace. The heat was terrible. Scampering across a gantry, the person slowed and turned as they reached a bank of water tanks.

'Watch out!' Jack yelled.

Bang!

They ducked as a bullet whizzed overhead. Mr Doyle produced his weapon, but held his fire as they charged down the corridor. Reaching a door to the outside, they carefully eased it open, but the intruder was nowhere to be seen.

'Gone,' Mr Doyle said. 'And now the plant is damaged.'

'But why?' Scarlet asked.

'This is a deliberate attempt to destroy the Darwinist League.'

'But it would kill the saboteur as well.'

'Maybe they're a fanatic,' Mr Doyle said. 'Or have some escape route of which we're unaware.'

'Do you think Fujita's behind it?' Jack asked.

'Him, or somebody like him.'

Reaching the control room, they found Blair had already assembled a crew who were examining the damaged consoles.

'Can they be fixed?' Mr Doyle asked.

'We think so,' a man answered. 'But it'll be touch and go for the next twenty-four hours.'

Returning to the hotel, Jack saw the lighting had already started to dim. By the time they reached their room, the city was in virtual darkness. As he peered out the window, Jack couldn't help but think of the thousands of tons of water pressed against the domes. If the walls should fail, even for a second, they would be crushed.

He had only just climbed into bed when there was a knock at his door.

'Jack?' Scarlet entered. 'I thought I'd join you, if that's okay.'

She climbed in under the blanket with him, and her body heat was like sitting near a fire on a cold winter's night.

'At least Hiro's not here,' she said.

'Do you have to mention him?' Jack snapped. 'At a time like this?'

'What do you mean?'

'You hang around each other like a pair of love birds!'

'I don't know what you're saying. He's not my boyfriend! I'm just glad he's not stuck down here with the rest of us to die!'

Scarlet suddenly burst into tears. Jack felt terrible. Everything she had said made sense. He took her hand.

'I'm sorry,' he said. 'I was stupid.'

'Yes! You were!' She wiped the tears away. 'I just want us to be away from here—and safe!'

Jack nodded. He lay back against his pillow, and listened to Scarlet's tears subside. After a moment, he realised her breathing was slow and steady.

I can't sleep, he thought. *I'm too worried to...*

The next thing he knew, he was diving into the ocean and descending rapidly, faster than a stone. A whale swam past with Mr Doyle and Scarlet on its back. They waved frantically to him.

'You must be careful!' Mr Doyle called. 'You take far too many chances.'

'If you see Brinkie,' Scarlet said, 'give her my best!'

It became more effortless the further Jack dived. Soon he reached the bottom where it was quiet and cool. Standing on a rocky platform, he looked up and saw the surface, miles away. But then he saw a huge shadow move across.

The Kusanagi sword can only be wielded by one who is true of heart and believes in its power.

When Jack opened his eyes next, he saw a pale-yellow light filtering through the window. Scarlet was still asleep. Jack sat up and saw illumination had returned to the city walls. The power station had come back to life, its faint murmur reverberating across Mizu City.

Thank goodness, Jack thought. *We're alive.*

CHAPTER TWENTY-ONE

Jack had never seen journalists in such a frenzy. After the murder, the diplomats and scientists had secreted themselves away with a joint policy of not speaking to the press. This led journalists to seek quotes from Mr Doyle. Mostly he fended them off, but when he did speak, he remained positive about Mizu City and the Darwinist League.

Privately, he told Jack and Scarlet of his fears. 'I just want to be out of this place,' he said. 'At least in Tokyo, we had a means of escape.'

With power returned to the city, Jack felt more relaxed. Whoever had sabotaged the plant had surely done all they could. Soon the diving bell would be operational again.

Edgar approached Jack and Scarlet as they did a tour of the Town Hall.

'*Hail to you, thane of Cawdor!*' he said, raising his arm. 'That's from the play that must not be named.'

'Er,' Jack said. 'Which one is that?'

'*Macbeth*,' Scarlet said. 'There's a superstition that if the name is mentioned, then all sorts of bad luck will follow.'

Jack glared at her. 'I hope you're not right,' he said. 'We've had enough bad luck already.'

'I once owned a copy of Shakespeare's first folio,' Edgar said. 'It was one of the most special times of my life.'

'I assume you stole it,' Scarlet said, coldly. 'A copy of Shakespeare's plays is priceless.'

'Not at all! I won it in a game of cards.'

'*A game of cards?*'

'I don't recommend gambling,' Edgar said, his face serious. 'It is a vile hobby, especially when you're losing. No, I was playing against one of the guards at the British Library and he was in some debt to me.'

'How much?' Jack asked.

'Two hundred and forty million pounds.'

Jack's mouth fell open.

'He had gambled foolishly,' Edgar admitted. 'I suspect alcohol had something to do with it. Anyway, I promised to call it even if he gave me the folio, and he agreed.'

'But it wasn't his to give,' Jack said.

'A small technicality. Anyway, I did not have it for long. The police raided my home soon afterwards and returned it to the library.' Edgar shook his head sadly. 'Anyway, I didn't come here to reminisce. I've had a word with one of the scientists so you can take a sneak-peak at something in one of the research labs.'

'What is it?' Scarlet asked, suspiciously.

'You'll see,' Edgar said, stifling a grin. 'Prepare to be impressed.'

They followed him to a long, rectangular building in Dome Four, where a huge fish tank with reinforced glass took up one entire wall.

Jack and Scarlet gasped.

'It's a whale!' Jack said.

'It is indeed,' Edgar said, smiling. 'I was able to talk Dr Livanov into letting us see her pet.'

Jack had never seen a whale, let alone one like this. It was blue-grey, and fifty feet long with tiny eyes. But the most peculiar thing was that most of its body was transparent.

'So it's one of the submarine-whales,' Scarlet said. 'Fascinating.'

A skinny man in a lab coat approached and introduced himself as Livanov's assistant, Harold Stackhurst.

'Would you like to see inside?' he asked.

He led them up a gantry and along the length of the creature before stopping at a hole in the top of the whale's head. A spiral staircase, made of skin-covered cartilage, led down. They descended fifteen feet to a large room with bench seats made of the same bony material. Looking out of the creature was like looking through a tinted blue window.

'And water can't get in?' Jack asked, nervously.

'The hatch isn't operational yet,' Stackhurst said. 'When it is, the interior will be as dry as a bone.'

He took them next to the bridge, he pointed at various controls: a single control stick that adjusted vertical and horizontal movement, and two foot pedals, one to accelerate and the other to brake. He explained that they were connected to the whale's central nervous system.

'Isn't it distressing for the whale?' Scarlet asked.

'This creature has no brain.'

'My goodness.'

'It's been bred without one.'

Scarlet poked around the creature for a while longer, but didn't find it as interesting as Jack.

'I'll see you up top,' she said.

He nodded. As Stackhurst led Scarlet out, Edgar took Jack aside.

'You know we may be able to use this creature,' he said.

'To do what?' he asked.

'Dr Livanov is in the final stages of preparing the creature for trials. It would be ideal to search the ocean floor for the sword.'

'But what about Mr Doyle?' Jack asked.

'My brother is a wonderful man, but he does not share our sense of destiny.'

'I'm not sure *I* have a sense of destiny.'

'You know what the Bard said? *Men at some time are masters of their fates*,' Edgar said. 'I was once wandering around the Stockholm Art Gallery when the power failed. There was a wonderful Degas picture on the wall. Do you know what I did?'

Jack could guess. 'You stole it?'

'I don't steal things. I just borrow them until someone else is able to acquire them back. You know my motto Jack: *Nobody owns anything.*'

'And what happened to the painting?'

'Taken by a criminal,' Edgar said. 'A foul man, he broke in while I slept, but as I say...'

'Nobody owns anything.'

'That's right.'

Before Jack could respond, Scarlet stuck her head down the stairs. 'Are you coming?' she called. 'Or have you moved in?'

Edgar said he wanted to stay and learn more about the whale and Jack headed back up on his own.

On the way back to the hotel, Scarlet asked Jack what Edgar had been speaking to him about.

'Oh, nothing,' he said, vaguely.

As soon as they reached the *Imperial*, it was clear something had happened. Mr Doyle was speaking to an agitated Einstein in the foyer.

'Ah,' Mr Doyle said, turning to them. His face was

grim. 'I'm glad you're here. There's been another murder.'

They followed the detective to a residential building in Dome One. In an apartment on the third floor, they found Blair standing over a dead man. Jack grimaced. No matter how many times he saw dead bodies, he never got used to it. The victim had also been killed with a knife.

'Who is this man?' Scarlet asked.

'Fingal Wilde,' Blair said. 'He's the new manager of Roads and Residential Development here in Mizu City.'

'Do you think he was killed because of his specialty?' Jack asked Mr Doyle. 'The same as Davidson?'

'I'm not sure why someone would be killed because of their knowledge of how to build a house or road.' He leant down, pointing to a small rectangular bloodstain on the floor. 'What do you make of this?'

'I'm not sure.'

Mr Doyle's eyes angled to Wilde's hands. Grasping one, he slipped on his goggles to examine it more closely. 'This makes no sense,' he murmured. 'These hands are rough.' Turning to Blair, he said, 'You say this man was a manager.'

'Yes.'

'Then why are his hands rough? Surely he wasn't a labourer.'

'That's probably from his previous job.'

'Which was?'

'Chief of the Waste Management Plant.'

'That's it!' Mr Doyle said, leaping to the feet. 'We

must not dawdle. Wilde wasn't killed because of his new job. He was killed because of his old one!'

They raced through the domes to the Waste Management building. A loud grinding came from the other end. The waste tray seemed to be in operation.

A man lay unconscious on the ground near its controls. Once again, these had been smashed beyond repair.

Mr Doyle quickly revived the man. Introducing himself as Tanner, the man pointed to the tray.

'The outer hatch has already started to open,' he said. 'The city will flood if we don't shut it.'

He tried manipulating the controls, but they were inoperative.

Tanner pointed to a panel inside the tray, just above the rubbish. 'There's an emergency locking system in the tray. The outer doors can be closed from there.'

'How do we get to it?'

'Someone's got to jump in.'

Jack grimaced. The tray was half filled with rubbish and salt water. He didn't relish climbing in, but it had to be done. Removing his green coat, he climbed onto the edge of the tray.

'Have a hot chocolate ready for me,' he said.

'Jack!' Mr Doyle started. 'Are you sure—'

Jack landed in the water and swam through the stinking water to the panel. Pulling it open, he peered in and saw the release lever. He tried turning it, but it wouldn't budge. The water continued to rise.

'Let me help you with that,' he heard Scarlet say from behind.

'What are you doing here?'

'Taking a bath!' she retorted. 'Did you really think I'd let you do this alone?'

They both gripped the lever. Resisting for another moment, it abruptly gave way. They heard a new machine kick into gear as a metal cover started to draw across the top.

'What's going on?' they heard Mr Doyle cry out.

'There's something wrong with the controls! The ejection system's activated. It's going to release into the ocean!'

'Well, stop it!'

Darkness enveloped Jack and Scarlet as the lid closed on the rubbish drawer. Beyond, they could still hear Mr Doyle and Tanner struggling to stop the machine. Jack gripped Scarlet's arm. 'Don't worry,' he said, trying to sound confident. 'They'll find a way to get us out.'

'I'm sure they will.'

The minutes passed. Finally they heard Mr Doyle banging on the lid.

'Can you hear me?' he yelled.

'Yes!' Jack called. 'What's happening?'

'We can't stop the ejection system. The controls are too smashed. But there's a slide drawer to your left. We're sending something down that can save you.'

Metal clanked and a faint light appeared as a slide drawer shunted open. Inside, they saw a lamp accompanied by two man-sized gelatinous lumps—one red, the other blue.

Grabbing the lamp, they shied away from the strange shapes.

'Jack,' Scarlet said. 'What are they?'

'I don't know!'

'Jack and Scarlet!' The voice came through the metal. 'It's Edgar! I've got Dr Hardy with me.'

Then Jack realised. 'Are these the jellysuits?' he asked. 'What are we supposed to do with them?'

'You need to swallow the breathing hoses,' Hardy yelled.

'Uh, thanks for the offer, but...'

'There's no other way! We can't stop the tray.'

Mr Doyle's voice again. 'Listen to me,' he said. 'You must use the jellysuits. Do as Hardy says. Once outside the city, you can re-enter via the airlock on the western side.'

Jack swam over to the creatures and shivered as he gently touched it. The creature felt like a warm water balloon. Pushing aside some blubber, he found the air hose. Like the tentacle of an octopus, it started twisting in his hand.

'Place the air tube into your mouth,' Hardy yelled. 'It will automatically make its way down your throat to your lungs. You will start breathing normally in seconds. The jellysuit will envelop you and you'll be able to safely swim outside the city.'

'What about the pressure?' Jack yelled. The water

had risen so high their heads were bobbing near the top of the tray.

'You will be protected,' Hardy replied.

Mr Doyle yelled again. 'You must do it!' he called. 'Or you'll die.'

Jack pulled the two creatures from the slide tray and it shunted shut. He dragged the red one over to Scarlet, whose face had gone white.

'Scarlet?' he said. 'Are you all right?'

'I can't do it,' she gasped. 'I can't put that thing into my mouth.'

CHAPTER TWENTY-TWO

'It will be fine,' Jack soothed. 'I know it seems revolting—'

'You can't make me do it.'

Scarlet drew back, utterly terrified.

'Scientists have tested these jellysuits,' Jack said. 'I know they seem odd, but they work.'

'I don't care,' Scarlet said, her eyes wide, staring at the strange creature. 'I can't do it.' As Jack swam closer, she splashed away from him. 'Don't force me! You can't force me!'

Jack remembered what she had said about almost choking as a child, and having a phobia about things being stuck in her throat.

'I'm not going to force you,' Jack said, keeping his

voice calm. 'But if you stay here, you'll drown.'

'I can't do it. The thought of that thing in my body...'

'Then we're both going to drown.'

Scarlet's eyes shifted from the creature to Jack's face.

'Because I'm not leaving you here,' Jack continued. 'If you decide to stay and drown, then I'm staying here too. But think of what it will be like for Mr Doyle. And for your father.'

For a long moment, the only sound was that of the water spilling into the tray. Then Scarlet focused on Jack as if awakening from a stupor.

'Of course,' she said, swallowing. 'But...you'll have to do it.'

Jack pulled the jellysuit towards Scarlet. Gathering her in his arms, he saw the fear again in her eyes.

I don't blame you, he thought. *The idea repulses me too.*

'Close your eyes,' he murmured. 'I promise I'll look after you.'

Forcing her eyes shut, she nodded. 'I know,' she said. 'Just make it quick.'

Scarlet hesitantly opened her mouth. Placing the air tube between her lips, he pushed it in.

At first, she was fine, but then she started to fight against him as the creature plunged down her throat. Her eyes bulged in horror.

'Breathe,' Jack urged her. 'Take long, deep breaths.'

Silently screaming, she clutched at him, but then closed her eyes and followed his instructions. Her chest rose and fell in panic, but slowly eased as her breathing turned to normal. When Scarlet opened her eyes, Jack saw no sign of panic. The creature shifted and cocooned itself around Scarlet.

Now it's my turn, Jack thought, releasing her.

He swam over to his blue jellysuit. There was no time to dally. The water was almost at his chin. Finding the breathing tube, he brought it to his mouth and gently sucked it in. An instant later he felt it pushing to the back of his throat.

No. Something's wrong. I can't breathe!

He struggled with the tentacle, trying to pull it back out, but now he felt a blubbery hand on his arm. Scarlet, fully encased in the jellysuit, gave him a reassuring smile.

Jack forced himself to breathe. The first breathe, he sucked in no air, the second, he received only half a breath, but by the time he breathed for the third time, he had a whole lungful.

All the time, Scarlet kept a hand on his arm to steady him as he learnt to breathe using the creature. It wrapped itself around him as the water reached the top of the tray. The lamp went out, but they were able to see as clearly as if it was day.

What was it Dr Hardy said? *We have added an enzyme that allows the wearer to see in virtual darkness...*

A shockwave moved through the water and the drawer tilted sideways. Before Jack could react, rubbish and churning water exploded past his face, sending him tumbling.

It was like being thrown about by the surf at the beach. Reaching out blindly, Jack grabbed a rock, and held on. It took him a moment to realise he was no longer in the city. The drawer had closed, depositing him under the curve of the city, and he was on the ocean floor. From close up, the nearest dome was like standing next to a mountain. Thousands of tiny fish chased scraps of food, and through them Jack saw domes receding into the distance.

I'm on the bottom on the ocean, he thought.

It was mind-boggling. It had all happened so quickly that he had not considered what it would be like. Now he understood what the first people to walk on the moon would feel.

Jack stood up unsteadily. Wearing the jellysuit, he felt neither hot nor cold, neither wet nor dry. His eyes scanned the ocean floor and he saw Scarlet slowly striding towards him. She gave him a wave, smiling.

She had a red tint to her as if he was looking through crimson glass. Around the top of her skull was a darker ridge, like a halo, but nothing to indicate joins in the skin.

Remembering his strange dream where Scarlet and Mr Doyle had ridden past on the back of the whale, Jack couldn't help but laugh.

They walked away from the city. The distant surface was miles above.

A powerful longing seized Jack as he stared past the domes. Hardy had said the suit would supply oxygen and protection from the pressure forever. Jack had a strange urge to walk across the ocean terrain forever, exploring, discovering new places that people had never before seen.

So how do we swim in these things?

Jack tried to freestyle, but only succeeded in arrowing towards the bottom. Scarlet found breaststroke to be far more successful. As they rounded the dome to the airlock on the western side, Jack glanced back across the ocean floor.

In the distance, so far away it looked like a star, he saw a glowing light. He blinked. The light was real, some sort of a metallic object giving off a constant, golden luminosity.

Scarlet grasped his arm. Jack looked at her and pointed, but she shook her head and pulled him towards the dome.

Let's go.

Reluctantly, he nodded. They kept to the western side, reaching an illuminated section under the city. Turning a wheel set into a circular hatch, they swam in and secured the door behind them. Another door slid open ahead and they stepped through.

Finally they stood on solid ground as the water was pumped out. A door opened above.

'Thank God!' Mr Doyle cried. 'You're alive.'

A dozen hands pulled them up. Within seconds they were gently extricated from the jellysuits, the breathing tube being the last part to be removed. Blankets were wrapped around them. Hot chocolate was supplied.

Hardy could barely contain himself. 'How was it?' he asked. 'What did it feel like? How—'

'Enough of that,' Mr Doyle snapped. 'Are you all right?'

'We're fine,' Scarlet told him.

'What about the city?' Jack asked.

'The Waste Management system is damaged, but repairable,' Mr Doyle said.

'I *must* question you later about the experience,' Hardy said.

Jack and Scarlet nodded, promising they would give him a full report. Mr Doyle insisted they return to the *Imperial* to change and eat.

An hour later, emerging from the restaurant, Scarlet took Jack aside.

'I need to thank you,' Scarlet said.

'What for?'

She looked at him incredulously. 'For saving my life!' she said.

'I do that all the time.'

'Not like this,' Scarlet said, reddening. 'I've never felt such blind terror in my life. I'm ashamed at my loss of control.'

'Everyone needs friends who can help them through hard times,' Jack said. 'But you can make it up to me.'

'How?'

'Try not to mention Brickie Blunderbuss for the rest of the time we're down here.'

'It's Brinkie Buckeridge—and I promise.'

He asked Scarlet about the glowing object on the ocean floor.

'It could have been some rubbish from when they built the city,' she said.

'Maybe.'

Later, Jack went in search of Edgar, and found him listlessly meandering through the park in Dome One. He brightened up when Jack told him about the glowing object.

'It must be the sword!' Edgar said. 'We should retrieve it at once!'

'But how will we get to it?' Jack asked.

'The diving gear, of course!'

'I doubt Mr Doyle or the other scientists would let us use it for a treasure hunt,' he said.

'Oh, they won't mind if we borrow it. We'll have it back before they even know it's gone.'

'I don't think—'

Bar-room!

The dome shuddered. Jack looked about in confusion. *What was happening?* He caught a glimpse of a large object moving past the dome wall.

'It's a submarine!' Edgar said. 'They must have fired a torpedo at the city.'

It sped past at high speed and disappeared from sight.

'Look!' Jack said, pointing. 'The dome!'

A hairline crack appeared in the wall and water began to gush in.

CHAPTER TWENTY-THREE

Chaos spread through the city. People began running in all directions as an alarm sounded.

Jack and Edgar hurried back to the hotel where they found Mr Doyle and Scarlet speaking to Einstein.

'We're evacuating the entire population to Dome Five,' Einstein explained. 'It's furthest from the point of attack.'

It only took minutes for most of the population to assemble in Dome Five. Many of the diplomats and journalists looked terrified, but Jack was relieved to see the scientists appeared calm.

Livanov went to the stage. 'We have seen an unprecedented attack on Mizu City,' she said. 'Dome One is rapidly filling with water. That means there is no way for us to access the diving bell. Without the diving bell, we can't return to the surface.'

An awful silence followed. Then several journalists began yelling questions at once.

'Can the diving bell be repaired from above?'

'Wasn't it designed for this kind of attack?'

'What about repairing the dome?'

Livanov called for silence. 'Whoever attacked knew exactly where to hit us,' she said. 'A section of Dome One was slightly damaged during construction. It was repaired, but has remained the weakest link in the entire city.

'That is where they attacked, which is why that section is now flooding. The dome could be repaired, but that would take weeks.' She paused. 'I should point out that a second attack at that section of the dome would destroy Dome One completely. We can survive in the remaining four domes, but the domes were not built to withstand sustained submarine attack.

'I'm sure rescue efforts are being made from the surface, but our submarine dock isn't operational. And the problem with the diving bell was from our end. If there is to be an escape from here, we must devise it ourselves.'

A great buzz began among the crowd as she left the stage. The scientists spoke together for several minutes before Hardy came over to Jack, Scarlet and Mr Doyle.

'I have a plan,' he said. 'There may be a way to return

everyone to the surface, but we'll need your help.'

'To do what?' Jack said.

'As you know, the domes are connected via lockable hatches,' Hardy said. 'Once locked, each dome becomes a self-contained sphere. Livanov's assistant, Harold Stackhurst, believes a dome could be towed to the surface by a whale.'

'What does Dr Livanov think?'

'That we should wait here until help arrives.'

Mr Doyle frowned. 'But surely one of these domes weighs thousands of tons,' he said. 'How can a single whale drag one to the surface?'

'The domes have natural buoyancy, but are secured to the seabed via an anchoring mechanism. Once disengaged, a whale would only need to give it the slightest tug to direct it to the surface. However,' Hardy added, 'there's one problem. The whale in the research lab has not been completed. The closing hatch is not installed, so the interior is not watertight. Two people in diving suits would need to steer it out of the city.'

'I thought normal diving suits wouldn't work at this depth.'

'They won't. Only people in jellysuits would be able to do it.'

'I see,' the detective said. 'And the only jellysuits...'

'...are the ones Jack and Scarlet have worn.'

'And no-one else can wear them.'

'We can do it, Mr Doyle,' Jack said. Turning to Scarlet, he added, 'Can't we?'

Jack was worried she might still be afraid of the jellysuit, but Scarlet nodded.

'We'll do it,' she said. 'Everyone's depending on us.'

Hardy returned to the scientists and spoke to them excitedly. The group soon walked over.

'You're very brave,' one scientist said.

'You deserve a medal,' another commented.

Livanov approached. 'I must tell you I'm completely opposed to this plan,' she said.

'Why?' Mr Doyle asked.

'I don't think it can work. We should wait here for help to arrive.'

'It may never arrive,' Mr Doyle said.

'We can do it,' Jack said. 'I know we can.'

After they had hurried to the whale research building, Stackhurst familiarised Jack and Scarlet with the controls. Then Hardy appeared with a length of thick chain.

'We'll disconnect the anchors from the bottom and Dome Five from the rest of the city. You'll find docking hooks around the hatch. The chain can be looped around those and tied to the whale's tail.'

'Are you sure you want to risk this?' Mr Doyle asked Jack and Scarlet again.

'We've been out there once,' Scarlet said. 'We can do it again. But I do have one request.'

'What's that?' Jack asked.

'I think I should do the driving,' she said. 'As you know, I have some experience.'

The one and only time Scarlet had driven a vehicle was when she drove a garbage truck down the main street of Margate, destroying dozens of vehicles.

'I'm not sure I'd call that a success,' Jack said.

'People *were* trying to kill us at the time,' she pointed out. 'And some experience is better than no experience.'

Sighing, Jack nodded.

The jellysuits were retrieved. Jack didn't feel as nervous this time as he and Scarlet took the suits into the whale. A cover was locked in place and the tank started to flood.

Jack watched Scarlet place the breathing tube into her throat again. A look of fear crossed her face, but quickly passed.

Good girl.

Jack slid the tube into his throat and a moment later he started breathing normally.

Water filled the cabin. It soon reached up to their shoulders and when the tank was filled, they felt the whale shudder momentarily and saw a door below it drop away.

Scarlet adjusted the control stick and they descended until the ocean floor appeared.

After rounding the dome with little difficulty, they soon found the hatch. People inside the dome gave them the thumbs up to indicate it was safe to proceed.

Jack left Scarlet at the controls while he grabbed a length of the chain and swam to the hatch. He knotted it tightly at one end before securing the other end to its tail.

Returning to the cabin, he nodded to Scarlet and she brought the control stick back. The whale slowly complied, pulling the chain tight. For one horrible moment, the whale shuddered and Jack thought the plan wouldn't work, but then the creature continued forward.

They ascended. Peering back at the city, Jack wondered how long it would take them to repair the damage done by the submarine. His eyes swept the ocean floor. He was missing it already.

I'll never forget standing on the bottom and staring up. It was like being on another planet.

Just as he was about to turn away, Jack saw a light. He pointed it out to Scarlet, but she was concentrating hard on the controls. Then the dome swung around and he lost sight of it. The whale continued.

An hour passed. Then two. Jack hoped everyone was all right. Hardy had instructed them to make the journey gradual. Everyone would get the bends if they ascended too quickly.

But Jack's impatience was getting the better of him. *Come on*, he thought. *We must be there soon!*

The surface never seemed to get any closer, but then Jack realised he could see more detail in the waves crashing above. Scarlet accelerated slightly. *Just a few more minutes. We're almost there.* Then the surface grew very bright and the whale broke through.

The dome slowly appeared, the top half bursting through the surface. Jack had forgotten how large it was.

Mizu Dock was about a mile away, a small fleet of Japanese navy vessels moored nearby. Scarlet angled the whale to one of the docking hatches where they removed the jellysuits.

'Do you think they're all right?' Jack asked.

'I'm sure they are,' Scarlet said. 'Look!'

Shapes were moving about near the hatch. It sprang open. A dozen faces appeared, including Mr Doyle, who leant out, waving.

'Well done!' he said. 'You've saved the day!'

'Has everyone survived?' Jack asked.

'I think so.'

Within minutes, people were evacuating to the navy ships. Dozens stopped to thank Jack and Scarlet for their efforts—even Dr Livanov.

'It seems I was mistaken,' she said, begrudgingly. 'We have you to thank for our lives.'

Mr Doyle took Jack and Scarlet to the bow of the ship as it cut through the water towards Japan.

'We'll be back in Tokyo within hours,' Mr Doyle said. 'Then we can concentrate on returning to England.'

Jack nodded, but his mind was miles away, on a glowing object on the ocean floor.

CHAPTER TWENTY-FOUR

Hours later, everyone involved with the Darwinist Symposium had been relocated back to the old jail in Tokyo.

Jack found it strange returning to the cell he had slept in only a few days before. He couldn't forget the experience of standing on the ocean floor, feeling like he was part of the sea.

As night fell over Tokyo, he stood at his cell window, staring at the deepening sky through the bars. Mr Doyle had announced they would leave late the next day, after cajoling Einstein into letting him make his closing address early. He had already sent a message to the prime minister, telling him it appeared the sword had been lost in a shipwreck centuries before and it was doubtful it would ever be recovered.

Jack felt sad. He didn't know when he'd visit Japan again—if ever.

'Jack?' Edgar appeared in the doorway. 'I hope I'm not interrupting you.'

'I was just thinking.'

'About what? The sword?'

It had been one of many things going through his mind. He told Edgar about seeing the sword.

'I know I didn't imagine it,' he said. 'It was there.'

'I'm sure you're right,' Edgar said. 'We must see for ourselves.'

'But we're leaving tomorrow.'

Edgar produced some cologne from his pocket and applied it liberally. '*Toulouse*,' he said. 'A lovely fragrance. Now, getting back to my brother. I know you have the utmost respect for him, as do I—but he doesn't believe in the sword.'

'Mr Doyle is right about most things.'

'But not always.'

'He said there were no ninjas in Japan,' Jack admitted. 'But the red ninja is real.'

'As is the sword,' Edgar said. 'As the Bard said, *Cowards die many times before their deaths. The valiant never taste of death but once*. Courage will enable us to find the sword and restore it to the people of Japan. The resulting alliance will keep England strong for decades, possibly centuries.'

'But how will we get to it?' Jack asked.

'You can use one of the jellysuits. I arranged to have both suits stored at the Mizu Dock,' Edgar said. 'Just in case.'

'Mr Doyle won't approve.'

Edgar held up a hand. 'My brother lacks imagination,' he said. 'That's not a criticism. It's a fact. He's so mired in logic and reason that he can't appreciate there may be more to the world than science.'

'I don't think—'

'We can leave early in the morning, and have the sword in our hands before he even knows we're gone,' Edgar said. 'We'll be back before breakfast.'

Jack thought about it. There was no way they'd be back before breakfast, but if they returned late with the Kusanagi sword, Mr Doyle would *have* to be impressed.

Prime Minister Kitchener had said there might be another war. Having Japan as an ally might save thousands—no—*millions* of lives.

'All right,' he said. 'I'll do it.' He didn't feel right about running around behind Mr Doyle's back, but it could mean the difference between war and peace.

'Good boy,' Edgar said, twirling his moustache. 'I'll wake you in the early morning. We'll be back before Ignatius has brewed his morning tea.'

Wishing Edgar goodnight, Jack climbed into bed, still thoughtful. He had never lied to Mr Doyle, but this wasn't really lying. It was simply omitting some information. That wasn't lying, was it?

Sleep did not come easily. Jack kept waking,

imagining Mr Doyle's disappointment at him disobeying his commands. He was still half-awake when he realised Edgar was standing in his doorway.

'We're ready, my boy,' he said. 'Time to make history.'

Jack threw some clothes on and, within minutes, was following Edgar to an exit.

Then Scarlet appeared in a doorway. 'What do you think you're doing?' she hissed at Jack.

'Go back to bed.'

'I'm not. Where are you two going?'

'We're retrieving the sword,' Jack said. 'I saw it on the ocean floor.'

'You saw *something* on the ocean floor.'

'We're trying our luck,' Edgar said. 'You're most welcome to join us.'

'I'd rather have all my teeth extracted.' She turned to Jack. 'Why are you doing this?'

'This is our last chance to find the sword. If it's never found, there might be another war. Do you want that?'

'Of course not.'

'Well?'

Edgar interjected. 'This will be much easier if you join us, my dear. A problem shared is a problem halved.'

Grumbling, Scarlet quickly dressed and followed them to a dragonfly that had been waiting on the roof.

'Good morning,' Hiro greeted them.

'You've been roped into this too?' Scarlet said.

'It sounds like we have a good chance of finding the sword.'

'Absolutely. We'll track down the Easter Bunny and Father Christmas while we're at it.'

They took to the air. It was still dark over Tokyo, although a million small fires had lighted the city. Jack shivered, pulling his green coat tight around him. He saw a glow on the horizon, signalling the dawn, as they left the coast behind.

Mr Doyle should be here, Jack thought. He felt bad that the detective was asleep in bed while he was on some secret mission to retrieve the sword.

This is all wrong. I never should have agreed to this.

But it was too late. Half an hour later, they were climbing out onto Mizu Dock.

By now, the sky was brighter, and the air warmer. A bank of black clouds ridged the horizon. It looked like another storm was on the way.

'We're in luck,' Edgar said. 'Not only has the city been abandoned, but also the dock. This whole area is now out of bounds.'

'So why are we here?' Scarlet said, sarcastically.

'As the Bard said, *Action is eloquence*. I once escaped a burning building by jumping from a window and grabbing hold of a giant pelican as it flew past. It carried me to safety.'

'I find that hard to believe.'

'Possibly it was *two* giant pelicans.'

Edgar led them to the dive building. It was deserted, but the two jellysuits lay in a tank.

He's got all this planned out, Jack thought. *What if I'd refused to go?*

The chain leading to the diving bell arrowed straight into the water.

'The sword is at the other end of that line,' Edgar said. 'Follow it to the city and you can orientate yourself to the sword from there.'

'*If* the sword is there,' Scarlet said.

Edgar nodded.

Still fully dressed, Jack and Scarlet slid into the water. Edgar handed them the jellysuits and they slipped them on.

'Don't take any unnecessary risks,' Edgar said, his voice sounding strange through the gelatinous skin of the jellysuit. 'And we'll see you in a few hours.'

Jack nodded. It was light outside the building. Mr Doyle would wake soon and wonder where they were.

I should have left a note, Jack thought. *He'll be worried sick.*

Sighing, he gave Scarlet a nod as they began their descent.

Swimming in the jellysuit was easier than ever. Jack felt like the creature could almost read his mind as he rapidly descended, using the chain as a guide. In the distance, he could just make out Mizu City. He glanced over at Scarlet. Smiling, she gave him a thumbs-up sign. She was doing fine.

Soon they arrived at Dome One. Peering through the skin of the city, Jack saw how the entire dome was now flooded. Personal belongings floated about inside, as well as squids and a school of fish.

How terrible, Jack thought. Turning to the ocean floor, he started over to where he had seen the glowing object.

It's gone. Someone's taken it.

Then his eyes caught a tiny flash of light, an object glistening about a mile away. Signalling to Scarlet, they swam towards it, Jack's excitement growing with every passing second. Finally, after being lost for centuries, the Kusanagi sword would again see the light of day.

Swimming between two rocky shelves on the ocean floor, they reached the shining object. Fish darted away in panic.

It looks different, Jack thought. *It was glowing earlier...*

The object—some sort of handle—was half-buried in the sand. Jack pulled on it, but the sword would not budge. Scarlet gripped the handle too and they tugged harder on it. It still wouldn't move.

What—?

A shadow passed overhead. Jack looked up in surprise to see a submarine. Then the sword's handle dragged him and Scarlet downwards as the water churned and sand exploded.

Too late, Jack realised the object wasn't a sword at all. It was the strut of a huge door. The submarine was descending into an underwater dock.

Jack and Scarlet tried to swim away, but the undersea

suction was too powerful. Desperately trying to avoid being crushed by the submarine, Jack watched helplessly as two doors slid across, closing them off from the ocean.

Water drained from the room, leaving the submarine in a shallow dock. Some lights flickered on.

Jack looked about for a way out, but they were caught between the submarine and a metal walkway. The submarine's hatch flew open and men with machine guns stormed out. A figure stepped out calmly after them.

'Welcome to my underwater city,' Fujita said.

CHAPTER TWENTY-FIVE

Jack and Scarlet had been dragged unceremoniously from the water, their jellysuits torn off them, and then taken to a cave. With so many guns trained on them, Jack couldn't see how they could escape.

'I demand that you release us,' Scarlet said. 'Or you will suffer the consequences.'

'Thank you for your advice,' Fujita said. 'But I will ignore it.' He smiled without humour. 'I thought you had escaped me, yet fortune has returned you.'

'What is this place?' Jack asked. 'And what do you mean about an underwater city? Mizu is the only underwater city.'

'Those Darwinists!' Futija said, his eyes darkening.

'What would they know?'

'According to science, the world must change,' Scarlet said, 'or we're doomed.'

Fujita laughed. 'What matters is the here and now,' he said. 'If a few forests disappear or a few animals become extinct, so be it. Only one thing lives forever—money!' He pointed to Jack and Scarlet. 'Take them to the dragon!'

Jack shot a glance at Scarlet.

The dragon?

They were pushed down a tunnel that opened up to a cavern the size of several football stadiums. It contained an underground city with apartment blocks adjacent to factories, streets and government buildings. Thousands of people could live and work here—but none did.

'What is this place?' Jack asked.

'The future,' Fujita said. 'The ideal city. A resident here need never leave the confines of my perfect world.'

Perfect world? It looks more like a jail, Jack thought. *Who would want to live here?*

But as they crossed the massive city, Jack couldn't help but be impressed by what Fujita had accomplished. Above this underground cavern were millions of tons of water. He had successfully engineered a submarine that could travel at these depths, as well as an underwater dock that could accommodate it. He had achieved the same goals as the Darwinists, but using steam technology.

Jack and Scarlet were forced down another tunnel. It opened out onto a cavern almost as massive as the first.

A scream caught in Jack's throat.

Directly before them stood an enormous creature with four squat legs as wide as the dome of St Paul's Cathedral. They were attached to a long, reptilian body, covered in metal scales, with bat-like wings sprouting from its shoulders.

The monster's claws were long and sharp, as were its teeth. Anything in that mouth would be crushed to pieces in seconds. At the other end of its body was a tail, large enough to demolish a city building with a single swipe.

'It's...' Jack finally found his voice. 'It's...'

'Not alive,' Scarlet said. 'It's a mechanical creature.'

Now that Jack peered more closely, he could see the wings were fixed in position, meaning it could not fly, but merely added to its terrifying appearance. Circular hinges connected the legs to its body, steam leaking from a dozen places.

The dragon's eyes were curiously blank. *The bridge must be up there*, Jack thought. *They must control it from there.* Tiny portholes were dispersed across its body where more of Fujita's men must have been stationed.

'Why?' Jack asked. 'What is this for?'

'Edgar Doyle was not successful in retrieving the sword,' Fujita said. 'Its power would have given me complete control over Japan. In the coming war, I would have kept Japan neutral. Once the other nations were weakened by war, I would have declared myself world leader, using the Kusanagi sword to destroy any who stood against me.'

His face darkened.

'But the sword has not been found. Possibly it never will be. So now I must use Plan B.'

'Which is?' Scarlet asked.

'The final destruction of the Darwinist League. Their dreams of clean energy will die with them.' Fujita pointed to Jack and Scarlet. 'Place them aboard the dragon,' he said. 'I wish them to see the destruction of Doyle and the others.'

Jack and Scarlet struggled against Fujita's men, but one produced a bottle filled with a foul-smelling potion. A soaked cloth was clamped over Jack's nose and the world swam around him.

When he next awoke, he was in a gloomy cell, his head aching.

'Scarlet?' he said.

Groaning, she lifted her head. 'Jack?' she said. 'Where are we?'

A distant engine chugged, and the room shuddered.

'I think that answers your question,' Jack said. 'We're on board Fujita's dragon.'

Scarlet's eyes widened. 'He said he was going to attack Tokyo!' she said. 'And the prison.'

Jack cursed himself.

Mr Doyle will be killed, he thought. *Why did I ever try to find the sword? We would have been on our way back to England by now.*

'This is all my fault,' he moaned.

Scarlet nodded glumly. 'It's not *all* your fault,' she

said, 'but it mostly is.'

'Scarlet—'

'What do you want me to say?' she snapped. 'You've followed Edgar Doyle around like a dog on a lead. Mr Doyle said he was a consummate liar, but you ignored him. Edgar doesn't have a moral bone in his body!'

Scarlet was correct in everything she'd said.

'All right,' he groaned. 'But now we need to get out of here and warn the others.'

'I've already been thinking about that,' Scarlet said. 'And I suggest we try the old-fashioned approach.'

Pulling out her lock pick, Scarlet had the door open in seconds. Creeping to the end of the corridor, they reached a T-intersection where they spotted a man guarding a door at one end.

'What will we do?' Jack whispered.

'Stay here and be ready,' she said.

Taking a deep breath, Scarlet stepped out into the hallway, stared at the man in shock and let out a little cry. She turned and ran in the opposite direction. Waiting until the man's footsteps had almost reached him, Jack stuck out his leg and tripped the man over. A punch to the jaw rendered him unconscious.

The dragon's engines changed pitch as Jack and Scarlet dragged the man back to their cell and locked him inside.

'It sounds like the dragon's almost ready to leave,' Scarlet said.

'We don't have much time,' Jack agreed. 'Do you have any thoughts about how to stop this thing?'

Scarlet frowned. 'This *does* remind me of a Brinkie Buckeridge book,' she said. 'She once had to stop a huge mechanical dragon from attacking Tokyo in *The Adventure of the Laughing Monster*.'

Jack's mouth fell open. 'You're joking.'

'I am,' she admitted. 'But I imagine attacking the bridge would be suicide.'

'Which leaves the engine room,' Jack said. 'Without power, this thing is just a lump of metal.'

The mechanical beast shuddered, and gave a huge lurch.

'We're moving,' he said. 'I just hope we're not too late.'

CHAPTER TWENTY-SIX

The motion of the metal creature reminded Jack of a roller coaster he had once ridden where he had been thrown about like a boat on a stormy sea.

Sea water dripped through cracks in the plating as the dragon lurched from side to side.

'Is this thing going to hold together?' Scarlet asked, as they were thrown against a wall.

'I hope so,' Jack said. 'Otherwise we'll need to learn how to breathe water.'

'Where do you think we are?'

'One of the legs,' Jack said, gripping a wall for support. 'Something of this weight can't swim. We must be walking to Tokyo.'

'So the engine room must be upstairs?'

'Probably in its belly.'

They continued their lurching climb up a spiral staircase to the next level. Water continued to seep through a thousand tiny joins.

This thing may look menacing, but it's barely holding together.

Reaching a dining hall, they saw a man at a stove in an adjacent kitchen. He was desperately trying to boil a pot of water. Tables had been bolted to the floor, but everything else—kitchen utensils, chairs and food supplies—were sliding everywhere.

'We should stop for a meal,' Scarlet whispered. 'I'm good with a pan.'

'I've eaten your cooking. I don't think so.'

Jack pointed to a door on the other side. They started across, but at that moment the pot fell off the stove. Cursing, the man grabbed for it—and spotted them. Screaming something in Japanese, he snatched up another pan and came towards them. Jack picked up a chair and hurled it, but the man knocked it aside.

Reaching Scarlet first, the man swung the pot. She ducked and slammed a fist into his stomach. Jack leapt onto one of the nearby tables, and slid across it as the dragon tilted, kicking the man between the legs, and followed up with a punch to the face. Grimacing, the man raised the pan, ready to bring it down on Jack's head.

Clang!

The man fell sideway, unconscious, revealing Scarlet with a frying pan.

'I said I was good with a pan,' she said.

'Are you all right?'

'I'm fine,' she said. 'Let's find the engine room and stop this thing.'

They continued through the creature, passing another porthole. Jack still saw only water, but it was lighter than before. *We must be nearing the surface.*

Reaching another corridor, he noticed the rise in temperature, and the sound of crackling ahead.

They spotted two men with empty wheelbarrows leaving a room, their overalls and faces black. The men returned a moment later, their wheelbarrows fully laden with coal.

'The engine room is through there,' Jack whispered, pointing to the first door.

Scarlet tilted her head. 'Do you hear that?' she asked.

The dragon's sounds had changed. Jack raced to the porthole at the other end of a storage room and saw a patch of blue sky, and the skyline of Tokyo.

'We're almost there!' he cried. 'How are we going to stop this thing?'

Scarlet frowned. Then her nose twitched. 'What's that smell?' she asked.

'It's not me!'

Her eyes focused on a nearby shelf. 'Look!' she said, pulling back a cloth. 'It's dynamite.'

'Bazookas!' Jack said. 'Fujita must have it for bombs.'

'A piece of this thrown into the furnace would cause the engine room to explode.'

'How do you suggest we get it there? Mail it?'

'I know!' Scarlet said, grabbing half-a-dozen sticks. 'Follow me!'

They raced up the corridor to the coal room. A couple of blackened overalls hung from pegs. Each dragging a pair on, Jack and Scarlet smeared coaldust over their faces and put on caps. Scarlet tucked her hair away.

'Are you sure this is going to work?' Jack asked.

'It worked for Brinkie Buckeridge in *The Adventure of the Singing Dachshund*.'

'We don't have a singing dachshund!'

'We don't need one!'

Jack tucked the dynamite down his overalls, and they made their way to the door of the engine room. The intense heat from the furnace stung the back of Jack's throat.

There were no lights other than the glare from the open door of the furnace. Before it, the men worked like a well-oiled machine: two transported coal across the room while two others shovelled coal into the furnace. A man monitored gauges on the engine while another listened to a speaking tube.

He barked an order and the men began to shovel more furiously. The sound of the enormous dragon changed again.

'We've hit land!' Scarlet hissed.

'We've got to blow the furnace up,' Jack said, 'but I don't see how.'

If they tossed the dynamite in, it would detonate immediately, killing them as well.

Jack snapped his fingers. 'I need a piece of cloth,' he said.

'What for?'

'To make curtains! Why do you think?'

Scarlet partially undid her overalls, and tore off a piece of her dress. Wrapping the dynamite, Jack smeared coaldust over it.

'There,' he said. 'It looks just like a lump of coal.'

'You've got a funny idea of what a lump of coal looks like!'

'It's close enough. Wait here.'

Jack studied the men. There was a tiny pause in their actions as the coal was poured from one wheelbarrow to the next. If he timed this right...

At the very instant their backs were turned, Jack scooted to the nearest coal bin, dropped the wrapped parcel into it and returned to Scarlet. He expected someone to raise the alarm, but no-one had noticed a thing.

Jack and Scarlet watched as the parcel was shovelled into a wheelbarrow and transported towards the fire.

'Come on,' Jack urged. 'Let's get out of here.'

Racing from the room, they ran straight into the

man who had left earlier. As he opened his mouth to shout, Scarlet knocked him out with a single punch.

'That was fantastic,' Jack said.

'Thank you,' she said. 'Now, come on. We haven't much time.'

They ran down the corridor, passing a porthole with a view over the city. The dragon had already carved a path of destruction through several suburbs of downtown Tokyo. Suddenly, the machine slammed into a skyscraper—and the building buckled.

Thousands of people will be killed! Jack thought. *No!*

But there was nothing he could do. He watched in horror as the skyscraper toppled like a mighty tree and slammed onto a hundred smaller homes, sending a plume of smoke and dust into the air. People ran in terror.

Scarlet dragged him away. 'We need to get away from the furnace before it blows,' she said.

They descended three more levels before Scarlet drew him into a storage room.

'We can hide in here,' she said.

Jack went to a porthole and looked out. 'Oh no,' he said. 'I know this part of the city.' He pointed. 'There's the jail.'

Scarlet peered over his shoulder. 'We're almost there!' she said. 'When will the dynamite explode?'

But nothing happened. Maybe the bomb had been discovered. A search could already be underway to find them. They would be discovered and the dragon would plough straight into the jail, killing everyone inside, including Mr Doyle.

Shoving aside a pair of office blocks, the dragon paused at the front gates of the jail.

We're failed, Jack thought. *And now Mr Doyle is doomed.*

CHAPTER TWENTY-SEVEN

Ka-boom!

Jack and Scarlet were thrown through the air. One explosion followed another as the furnace exploded.

We did it, Jack thought. *We've stopped the dragon.*

Then shelves toppled onto him and he was knocked senseless.

When he woke, smoke and the smell of burning metal filled the air.

Where am I?

He remembered: the engine room must have been destroyed and the dragon disabled.

'Scarlet?' he called.

He could see rain through a hole torn in the wall.

Nearby, Scarlet groaned. 'Jack?' she said. 'I'm under the shelving. I can't move.'

Struggling to his feet, Jack began frantically pulling shelves away. When he was finished, Scarlet gingerly stood, rubbing her head.

'I'm looking forward to a nice long bath when all this is over,' she said.

They edged through the break in the wall onto the roof of a cell block a few feet below.

Jack peered back at the dragon. The machine had fallen sideways across the prison, crushing several buildings. Critically wounded in the explosion, a huge hole had been blasted in its stomach, and smoke and steam poured from it.

Beyond, through the rain, Jack saw a path of destruction had been carved through the centre of Tokyo. Hundreds of buildings were either crushed or shattered beyond repair. Even as Jack watched, a city block finally gave way, collapsing into a heap and sending dust into the air. Fires burned, but the downpour was already reducing them to spindly smoke. Distant screams echoed across the city.

'Come on,' Scarlet said, gently. 'We need to find Mr Doyle.'

They pulled at roof tiles. Creating a hole, they climbed through to the attic of the jail. They came out at an administrative section packed with dusty files and old desks.

They weaved through the building to ground level.

Heading across the exercise ground, they heard a cry.

'Jack! Scarlet!'

Mr Doyle ran towards them and scooped them up in a hug. 'Where on earth have you been?' he demanded. 'Were you with Edgar? And what—'

Jack interrupted, explaining everything that had transpired over the day.

Mr Doyle's face grew darker as he listened to the chain of events. 'That brother of mine has been an anchor around my neck for the last time!' he said. 'I never want to see him again!'

'I'm sure he meant for the best,' Jack started.

'The best?' Mr Doyle was furious. 'He almost got you and Scarlet killed just to find a magical sword! When I see him—'

Scarlet laid a hand on Mr Doyle's arm. 'Please,' she said. 'This should wait. There must be people who are injured and require help.'

'Of course,' Mr Doyle said, swallowing. 'You're right.'

They went into the main section of the jail where a makeshift hospital had been set up by several of the Darwinists. Many of the diplomats and their staff were already collecting injured people from the streets.

Einstein waved over Jack and the others.

'There's a school down the block,' he said. 'Several children are trapped inside.'

Jack, Scarlet and Mr Doyle raced through the downpour to the collapsed building. People were already climbing out from ruined homes and shops. The sounds of sirens cut across the rain, but Jack knew there couldn't be enough emergency vehicles for a disaster of this scale.

The school, a timber structure, had been knocked sideways by the dragon. A boy was in the process of struggling out from under some beams when they arrived. Jack helped him out.

Mr Doyle spoke to the boy in Japanese before turning to Jack and Scarlet.

'There are more children inside,' he said. 'But this is too tight a fit for me to get through.'

'I can get in,' Jack said.

He squeezed his head into the gap. Ten feet below, in the gloom, a dozen faces looked up at him.

'Hello,' he said. 'Are you all right?'

The children were young—no older than eight or nine. It was clear they didn't understand English.

'My name's Jack,' he said, deciding his voice might calm them. 'I'll get you out of here.' He pointed up at the gap, and indicated food and drink lay at the other end. 'Mmm,' he said, rubbing his stomach. 'Yummy food. Nice drinks.'

Despite the terrible circumstances, one child burst out laughing.

'All right,' Jack said. 'I never said I was an actor.'

Slowly and methodically, he lifted each of the children up through the hole until only one remained.

'Now it's our turn,' Jack said.

The boy shook his head, afraid, and said something in Japanese.

Mr Doyle's voice came down through the gap. 'Jack,' he called, concern in his voice. 'This building seems quite unstable. I suggest you hurry.'

'I'm on my way,' Jack called. Turning to the boy, he said, 'We need to go.'

The boy pointed to a corner of the room where the ceiling had collapsed. Jack went over. There was nothing to see except some wire cages.

Meow.

'I see,' Jack said. Most of the cages were partially crushed, and mercifully empty, but one held a small black and white kitten. After scooping it out, Jack lifted him to the gap. Taking a breath of fresh air, the kitten scampered up and out.

Next Jack lifted the boy into his arms as the building gave an ominous groan. He pushed him ahead.

'Go up,' he urged. 'Keep moving.'

Despite his lack of English, the boy followed his directions. A crash came from somewhere within the debris.

As he crawled after him, Jack saw a timber beam over the boy's head start to shudder, and he held it up as it started to sag.

'Go!' Jack screamed. 'Quick!'

'Jack!' Mr Doyle called, as the boy escaped. 'Come now!'

'The beam is resting on my back,' Jack gasped. If

222

he moved, the whole thing would come down on him, crushing him to death. 'I can't move.'

Mr Doyle cursed. Jack heard movement at the other end. Then he saw Scarlet pushing herself through the gap.

'No,' Jack groaned. 'Stay where you are.'

'And leave you? Don't be ridiculous.' She had a short length of wood in her hand. Within seconds, she had jammed it under the beam. 'Mr Doyle,' she said. 'You must grab my legs and be ready to pull me back. I will be holding Jack.'

The makeshift support had taken most of his weight, but Jack doubted it would hold.

'No,' he grunted. 'You've got to leave me.'

'One more word out of your mouth,' Scarlet said, 'and I'll regale you with the plot of every Brinkie Buckeridge novel.'

Jack shut up.

Scarlet grabbed Jack's hands. 'I'm ready,' she said.

'On the count of three,' Mr Doyle said. 'One... two...three!'

The beam gave a mighty groan as Jack was jerked away from it. A second later he, Scarlet and Mr Doyle were in a pile on the street as the structure collapsed.

'My boy!' Mr Doyle cried as they climbed to their feet. 'Are you hurt?'

'I'm fine, sir. Just a bit roughed up.'

Fire officers approached them. Mr Doyle explained what had happened and the men started an examination of other buildings. The rain gradually eased and stopped. The skies over Tokyo became a buzz of activity as emergency services arrived from all over the country.

'I suggest we return to the jail,' Mr Doyle said. 'They may need our help.'

They spent the rest of the evening helping the scientists tend to the wounded. Ambulance officers arrived to take away the most severely injured.

The police arrived to do a full examination of the dragon's remains. One of them, a detective by the name of Hara, questioned Jack and the others. He listened in silence as Jack explained everything he and Scarlet had seen, leaving out details about the Kusanagi sword.

Hara laughed nervously. 'You say Mr Fujita controlled this mechanical monster,' he said. 'But he is a respected businessman.'

'He has an underground city,' Scarlet said. 'And admitted to attacking the Darwinist League.'

'That can't be true.'

Jack's eyes almost popped out of his head. 'It can't be true?' he said. 'We just told you it's true.'

Detective Hara turned to Mr Doyle. 'Your children have active imaginations,' he said. 'They like adventure stories.'

Mr Doyle turned bright red. 'I assure you that my assistants are not making this up,' he said. 'Fujita is a dangerous criminal and must be arrested—immediately.'

Hara smiled pleasantly. 'We will look into it.'

Jack was ready to explode by the time Hara walked

away. 'What is wrong with that man?' he asked. 'Is he deaf?'

'Not deaf,' Mr Doyle said. 'But you recall Hiro said crime families are very powerful here in Japan.'

'So you're saying Hara's afraid?'

'Or doesn't like facing the truth.'

Fortunately, the part of the jail where Jack and the others were staying was spared from the attack. As they wandered across the lobby, they heard a cry and turned to see Edgar racing across the foyer with Hiro close behind.

'Jack! Scarlet!' Edgar called. 'Are you all right?'

Mr Doyle looked like he wanted to throttle his brother. 'They're as well as can be expected!' he said. 'Considering you almost got them killed!'

'I don't know what—'

The detective grabbed him by the lapels. 'The only person you've ever cared about is yourself,' he said. 'You almost cost Jack and Scarlet their lives. We're leaving Japan tomorrow and I never want to hear from you again!'

Hiro gently eased them apart. 'Please,' he said. 'You are brothers. You must not fight.'

Edgar, ashen-faced, looked down. 'I'm sorry,' he said. 'I just wanted to find the sword.'

'Don't you understand?' Mr Doyle said. 'There is no such thing as a magic sword. The only things that matter are science and reason.'

'I did not mean any harm.'

'All you've ever done is cause harm. You owe both Jack and Scarlet an apology.'

'Of course,' Edgar nodded. 'I apologise, Jack, and to Scarlet too, wherever she is.'

Mr Doyle peered around. 'Scarlet?'

'She was here a moment ago,' Jack said. 'I'm sure she'll turn up.'

But she didn't.

CHAPTER TWENTY-EIGHT

'It was while we were arguing,' Mr Doyle said. 'I never should have taken my eyes off her.'

Jack, Mr Doyle, Edgar and Hiro were in the dining room of the jail. They had spent the previous night turning the place upside down, trying to find Scarlet.

Nothing.

The next day, they had searched the neighbourhood. Late in the afternoon, one of the scientists found her purse in an alley behind the building. Quizzing a young boy in a nearby restaurant, he told them he had seen a steamcar speeding away with a red-headed girl in the back.

'She's been kidnapped,' Jack said.

'We don't have evidence of that,' Edgar said.

'Then what do you think has happened?' Mr Doyle asked.

Edgar remained silent.

'It's all my fault,' Jack said as tears splashed down his face. 'I wish I'd never gone searching for that stupid sword!'

Mr Doyle laid a hand on his shoulder. 'We will find her,' he said. 'I promise.'

A bellhop arrived with a message. After reading it, Mr Doyle turned to them grimly.

'There is to be a meeting,' he said, 'at the Imperial Palace. Only Jack and myself are allowed to attend.'

'Who's the letter from?' Edgar asked.

'There's no name,' he said, 'but who do you think?' *Fujita*.

'But why kidnap Scarlet?' Jack asked. 'It doesn't make any sense.'

'I don't know either,' Mr Doyle said.

'We need to tell the police.'

'The note says that Scarlet will be harmed if we approach the authorities. The best thing we can do is handle this on our own.'

The meeting was set for eight o'clock the next morning. Mr Doyle insisted that everyone retire to bed early. Space was found for Hiro and Edgar in adjoining rooms.

As Jack climbed into bed, he heard a knock at the door.

'May we speak?' Hiro asked, entering.

'Sure.' Jack was exhausted beyond words. 'What is it?'

'You did not like me when we met.'

Jack swallowed. 'I'm sorry,' he said. 'I should have treated you better.'

'Why were you so defensive? Was it because of Scarlet?'

'I suppose so.'

'We went out a few times, taking in the sights of Tokyo. We spoke of many things, but her conversation always returned to you,' Hiro said. 'She greatly admires you. You are her world.'

'I don't think that's true.'

'It *is* true. You are in her thoughts at all times,' he said. 'Day and night. She is not alone, even now, because you are thinking of her. Nor are you alone. She is with you, always.'

After Hiro bid goodnight, Jack sent a message out into the dark.

Hold on, he thought. *Hold on, Scarlet.*

The next morning, Jack woke and was dressed before the sun rose. He found Mr Doyle already in the living room, checking his gun.

Edgar and Hiro had made breakfast for them, and insisted they eat. But the food tasted bland to Jack. Nothing had any colour while Scarlet's life was in danger.

Mr Doyle found a steamcab that took them through the busy metropolis. To Jack's surprise, most of the city was operating normally, despite the massive devastation that had occurred. Businesses were running. People were heading to work. Children were going to school.

The Japanese Imperial Palace was a rambling, wooded area, crowded with ancient buildings. Mr Doyle paid the fare and the steamcab chugged away.

'Mr Doyle,' Jack said. 'What if...how do we know Scarlet is even...?'

'Alive? That scoundrel kept my useless brother alive for weeks. Scarlet is a far more valuable asset, and Fujita is a businessman. He will do nothing to harm her.'

They arrived in the East Garden. Following signs written in both Japanese and English, they reached the meeting place, a small bridge over a pond.

'I'm sorry all this has happened,' Jack said.

'Don't blame yourself,' Mr Doyle said. 'My brother has fooled and cajoled far more experienced people into following his crazy schemes. He was arrested once for selling London Bridge.'

'You're joking.'

'I wish I was. He'd sold it to more than a dozen people, including the American ambassador and the King of Spain, before the police closed in.'

A figure appeared from some nearby trees. Jack gasped as a woman crossed the lawn towards them.

'Good morning,' Dr Livanov said. 'It seems we meet again.'

'You!' Jack said. 'You're working with Fujita!'

'Better to be on the winning side than the alternative.'

'I knew a woman was responsible for the sabotage

at Mizu City,' Mr Doyle said, turning to Jack. 'You remember the rectangular bloodstain at Fingal Wilde's murder? It was a woman's heel.'

'Very clever,' Livanov said.

'I assume you were also responsible for the explosion on board the *Katsu*, and the other deaths.'

'Guilty as charged,' Livanov said. 'I have sweated and toiled my entire life in the name of science, and you know what it has gotten me? Nothing!'

'I thought you loved science,' Jack said.

'I did,' she said, 'for many years. And then I saw friends and family buying big houses and private airships, while I had nothing. I lived in a small flat without heating and with little food. Now all that will change.'

'What has Fujita promised you?'

'My own tower in the heart of Tokyo and so much money I could never live long enough to spend it all.' She paused. 'But we're not here to speak about me.'

She handed an envelope to Mr Doyle. He opened it to reveal a strand of thick red hair.

'Where is Scarlet?'

'Safe,' Livanov said. 'For now.'

'What does Fujita want in return?'

'You know what he wants.'

'The Kusanagi sword? We don't have it.'

'But he believes you can find it. When he picked up Jack and Scarlet on the ocean floor, he didn't have time to question their reason for being there. Only later did he realise they were not looking for him.

They were seeking the sword.'

'So why doesn't he try to find it?'

'Fujita needs to keep a low profile for now. The police have been asking unfortunate questions.'

'Even if we could produce the sword,' Mr Doyle said, 'it's just an artefact. A lump of metal.'

Livanov shrugged. 'You and I are people of science,' she said. 'Fujita still believes in fairy tales and magical swords. What he wants, he gets.'

'You will both pay for your crimes!'

'That's unlikely. You have forty-eight hours to retrieve the sword, and bring it to Fujita's penthouse.'

'And if we can't locate it?'

'That would be unfortunate.'

Jack took a step towards the woman, but Mr Doyle restrained him as she calmly walked away and disappeared among trees.

He turned to Mr Doyle. 'What are we going to do? We don't have the sword.'

'I know.'

Jack's mind churned. 'There is something we can do,' he said. 'We have a map showing its location. I can find it.'

'But you already searched the ocean floor.'

'No,' Jack said. 'When I first saw the sword, it was *glowing* on the bottom. Later, I mistook light *reflecting* off Fujita's submarine base for the sword. They were two different things. The sword is still there.'

Leaving the Imperial Palace, they were amazed to

see Edgar and Hiro waiting on the street for them.

'What do you want?' Mr Doyle asked Edgar, scowling.

'I want to help,' Edgar replied.

'As I do,' Hiro added.

Mr Doyle grudgingly explained what had happened.

'I never trusted that Livanov woman,' Edgar said. 'Her perfume was *horrendous*, as if someone had drained a gutter and bottled it.' He nodded thoughtfully. 'Jack is right about the sword; recovering it is the only way to satisfy Fujita and save Scarlet.'

'But surely the police—' Mr Doyle started.

'This isn't England, Ignatius. It would take days—or weeks—to get a warrant to search his tower, and Scarlet will be long gone by then.'

Mr Doyle sighed. 'I can't believe we have to put our faith in finding an imaginary sword,' he said.

'How do you know it's imaginary?'

'Because there's no such thing as magic.'

'Ignatius, do you remember when I first moved into your house? When our parents were married?'

'How could I forget?'

'You may think that was a terrible time for you, but it was for me also. After my father died, I thought I could not go on.' Edgar fixed Mr Doyle with a steely glance. 'But then I met you and your father, and it changed my life. I was given hope. It can't be measured, quantified or proven, and yet we all live with it every day of our lives.'

Thoughtfully, Mr Doyle nodded.

Hiro took them to the roof of a nearby building where he had a dragonfly ready. Soon, they had left the city behind and were arcing across the ocean towards Mizu Dock.

'I'll need a jellysuit to get to the bottom,' Jack said.

'Never fear,' Edgar said, pulling open a trunk. 'We have two.'

'Where—'

'They're your suits. I found them in the wreckage of Fujita's dragon.'

'You stole them.'

'Not at all. I *found* them.'

Reaching the dock, Edgar and Hiro carried the trunk inside.

'Be careful,' Mr Doyle told Jack. 'If you don't have any success, return to the surface and we'll formulate another plan.'

Hiro shook Jack's hand. 'There is an old saying,' he said. 'Beware the hungry sea. It has an endless appetite.'

'I'll watch my step.'

Slipping on the jellysuit, he climbed into the water. The others wished him good luck and he started down.

From here on, Jack thought, *I'm on my own.*

CHAPTER TWENTY-NINE

Jack followed the chain towards the ocean floor.

He remembered Hiro's words: *Beware the hungry sea. It has an endless appetite.*

Stopping only once, he turned, looking back at the dock, now only a tiny square floating in the ocean.

I have never been this alone before.

He thought of his parents as he continued downwards. Never in their wildest dreams would they have imagined he would swim to the bottom of the ocean. His father was a poor swimmer, and his mother couldn't swim at all.

Finally he sighted the underwater city and found the spot where he had seen the glow. His eyes swept the bottom, but there was no sign of it.

Maybe the submarine churned up the sand.

Jack swam in the direction where he thought it was, but only succeeded in drawing perilously close to Fujita's underwater city.

A huge section of the ocean floor had been disturbed. *What happened here?* Then he realised: this was where an airlock had opened to release the dragon. The sand had been completely upturned. What if the sword had been buried forever?

He was beginning to feel panicky until he spotted something to his left, an odd shape in a sandy hollow. A sunken ship? Swimming over, he realised it was very ancient, the bow reduced to skeleton ribbing, the rear covered in sand.

Entering the wreck, Jack searched the gloom for signs of the glowing sword, but it was empty. Anything it had held had been long since claimed by the sea. As he headed towards the stern, he spotted a school of fish darting away in panic, and an octopus disappeared between some decking.

A shadow moved overhead, a ten-foot fish.

That's no fish, Jack realised. *That's a shark.*

He stayed completely motionless. A book he'd read said sharks had excellent vision, but if he remained still, it wouldn't detect him. After it had disappeared into the distance, Jack relaxed, his foot hitting against something. A piece of metal.

Picking it up, he saw instantly that it wasn't the

sword, just a piece of bracing from the ship. Jack cursed silently to himself.

It might take years to find—

Wham!

The shark slammed into him from behind, throwing him through the hull, the bracing still in his hand. He swung about desperately, trying to hit the shark, but the metal was knocked away.

Bazookas!

The jellysuit had saved his life, but the shark had damaged it. Already, a large section was starting to turn purple. If the suit failed down here, the water pressure would crush him in seconds.

The shark turned, making a wide circle around Jack. The city was about a mile away. He had to return to the diving chain if he stood any chance of surviving, but he had to deal with the shark first.

What else did that book say about sharks? If attacked, aim for the face, eyes or gills, which had all seemed very reasonable while curled up in the library at Bee Street. Doing it in real life was far more difficult.

The shark came at him like a missile. Jack stabbed at the creature, striking a glancing blow as it spun him around. While the shark disappeared behind the hull, Jack struggled to his feet again. The jellysuit was now mauve in three spots.

I'm finished if it attacks again.

Appearing from behind a rock ledge, the shark

rounded the wreck. Jack stabbed at its left eye, following up with a second blow to its gills.

The shark recoiled in pain. Jack had dealt it a painful blow, extinguishing all thoughts of using him as a meal, and it shot away.

Jack realised he was finding it hard to breathe, but not from fear. The suit was now bruised purple in half-a-dozen places.

I've got to get out of here—now!

He swam back towards Mizu City while trying to slow his heart rate and keep his breathing calm. Stress would only increase his blood circulation and need for oxygen.

At last he reached the diving bell, gripped the metal chain and glanced back one final time at the ocean floor. A few hundred feet away, nestled between sand banks, was a glowing object. Jack recognised it immediately.

He slowly crossed the sea floor to find a four-foot long case.

This is it, Jack thought. *This is the Kusanagi sword.*

Made from silver, the case had tarnished over the years, but still had Japanese lettering etched onto the surface.

Easing it from the sand, Jack couldn't find an opening, but at least it had a handle.

Jack swam back to the diving chain, dragging the case behind him. The chain above seemed to go on forever. Grabbing a piece of seaweed, Jack tied the case around his waist and started up.

This will take ages, he thought. *But I can't focus on that. I've got to concentrate on Scarlet.*

He kept swimming, but had only covered a short distance when a wave of dizziness overcame him. The bruising on the jellysuit had worsened, turning black in several places.

The creature was dying.

Jack couldn't help but feel sad. Hardy had called it a symbiotic relationship, but it had really all been one-way. What had Jack done for this strange life form? It had saved his life numerous times, and now it was dying.

Just a little further, he thought. *Please.*

He continued up the side of the chain. The case was a dead weight with no streamlining to make it easier to move through the water. He may as well have been towing a sledgehammer.

How much further?

His breath was laboured now, as if he'd run a marathon.

What had Hiro said to him about Scarlet?

She is not alone, even now, because you are thinking of her. Nor are you alone. She is with you, always.

Gripping the chain, Jack used it to climb up like a monkey, his vision blurring. Most of the suit had turned black in its last moments of life.

I can't do it, he thought. *I'm not going to make it.*

But then a huge shape appeared next to him. For one terrifying moment, Jack thought the shark had returned, but the massive bulk didn't attack. Through hazy vision, he realised it was the whale he and Scarlet had used to tow the dome to the surface. Mr Doyle had said it had gone missing after saving them.

The whale gently bumped him, like a dog nudging a child. Jack managed to cling on as the creature lifted its head and headed towards the surface.

The water broke and churned, and then Jack was bathed in sunlight. He was only dimly aware of Mr Doyle and the others as they dragged the jellysuit from him. All he could focus on was breathing, and the warmth of the sun.

His senses only fully returned when he saw Mr Doyle about to push the dying jellysuit over the edge of the dock.

'No,' Jack choked, vomiting up water.

'I'm afraid the creature's finished,' Mr Doyle said. 'I'm sorry.'

Saying a silent prayer, Jack gave the jellyfish one final embrace before rolling it over the side of the dock. It splashed into the water, and rapidly disappeared, consigned forever to the hungry sea.

CHAPTER THIRTY

It took Jack a minute to realise Edgar was cheering. Slowly rising to his feet, Jack watched the man in amazement as he literally danced for joy. Mr Doyle shook his head sadly. Hiro just stared.

'We've done it! No!' Edgar said, pointing at Jack. '*You* did it! Jack, you've solved one of civilisation's greatest mysteries.'

'Don't count your chickens yet,' Mr Doyle warned. 'We don't know what's in that case.'

'What else can it be?' Edgar asked. 'It must be the sword.'

Hiro tried the latches. 'These are difficult to move,' he said. 'I will need a knife.'

Going through his pockets, Mr Doyle pulled out a lump of cheese, a teddy bear, three onions and a brass elephant before producing a penknife.

Hiro applied it to the latches. After a minute, he gave a satisfied grunt.

'I have it,' he said.

They grouped around as he levered up one latch, and then the other.

'This is it,' Edgar said. 'History in the making.'

Hiro raised the lid.

'Oh dear,' Mr Doyle said. 'That's unfortunate.'

The interior of the box was in good condition, lined with some kind of wood. An indentation showed where the sword had lain, but it was no longer there. All that remained was its handle.

Hiro gently lifted the handle from the box. 'This is the *tsuka*—the hilt—of the sword,' he said. 'But the rest is gone.'

'Where?' Edgar asked, stupidly. 'I mean...why isn't it here?'

The handle was slightly curved and wrapped in some kind of skin, with a semi-circular guard to protect the swordsman's hand.

'This is shark skin,' Hiro said, fingering the skin. 'And the guard is of the highest quality. This *is* the Kusanagi sword.'

'But the blade...' Edgar's voice trailed off.

'Gone,' Mr Doyle said, sighing. 'Lost to history hundreds of years ago. I doubt it'll ever be found. But that's not the worst of our problems.'

Jack swallowed. 'Fujita won't accept this?'

'A handle? I doubt it,' Mr Doyle said. 'We'll need another plan. Edgar?'

Edgar, still staring in dismay at the handle, roused himself. 'Of course,' he said. 'Another plan. We still need to save Scarlet.'

'We could attack the tower,' Hiro said, almost to himself. 'But our chances of success would be small.'

'Fujita only has to give the word,' Edgar said, 'and Scarlet will be killed.'

'If she hasn't been already,' Jack said, sadly.

'She's alive. Fujita is a businessman. I suspect he is more than happy to exchange her for the sword.'

'But we don't have a sword,' Jack said. 'We have a handle.'

'We wouldn't insert another blade into it?' Mr Doyle suggested.

'Not into this,' Hiro said, examining it closely. 'It would take a craftsman weeks to create the blade.'

'And we don't have weeks,' Edgar said. 'We need to hand him the Kusanagi sword.' He frowned. 'Or something that looks very much like it.'

'Edgar?' Mr Doyle said.

'There is a sword in the Japanese Museum known as the Moon Blade. It is almost a thousand years old. There would be very little difference between it and the Kusanagi sword.'

'But it's in the Japanese Museum.'

'At the moment.'

'At the...' Mr Doyle's voice trailed away. 'You're not suggesting we break in?'

'That's exactly what I'm suggesting.'

'And steal the Moon Blade?'

'You know how much I hate that word,' Edgar said, taking out a bottle and spraying on some cologne. 'They would simply be lending it to us.'

'Like others have *lent* things to you over the years?'

'You know what I always say. Nobody—'

'—owns anything. Yes, you've been spouting that particular piece of logic for years.' Mr Doyle's eyes narrowed. 'You've been planning this for some time. Haven't you?'

'What do you mean?'

'Robbing the museum.'

Edgar reddened. 'Let's just say that I've explored the possibilities. As the Bard said, *Ignorance is the curse of God; knowledge the wing wherewith we fly to heaven.* A man must keep his mind active otherwise it atrophies.'

'Can we do it?' Jack asked. 'Will Fujita be fooled into thinking the Moon Blade is the Kusanagi sword?'

'He will be fooled long enough,' Edgar said. 'And that's what's important.'

'I can't believe we're even discussing this,' Mr Doyle said. 'Breaking into the Japanese Museum! And stealing a priceless artefact to hand over to a crime boss! It's insane!'

'But necessary,' Hiro said. 'Scarlet's life depends on us carrying out this subterfuge.'

'You know what will happen if we don't try,' Jack said to Mr Doyle.

The detective glumly nodded.

Climbing back onboard the dragonfly, Mr Doyle and Edgar chatted while Jack stared out the window. His thoughts were with Scarlet. Was she being looked after? Were her captors treating her well?

The sun was setting by the time they reached Tokyo. Edgar told them he had a detailed plan, but would need some supplies. He told Hiro to take them to a safehouse he had on the outskirts of the city.

After disappearing inside, he returned with a backpack and a change of clothing: blue leather pants, a matching coat and a leather top hat.

'Should I enquire as to where you got that clothing?' Mr Doyle asked.

'Probably best if you don't.'

Edgar then directed them to a hotel opposite the Japanese Museum.

After Mr Doyle rented a room on the top floor, he bought everyone dinner, which they ate as the sun set.

Jack was mostly silent during the meal, but Edgar was happy to chat cheerily about his various exploits.

'Oh, but there have been some close shaves,' he said. 'One time I was pursued by over a dozen armed Russian soldiers over a little matter of the crown jewels. If I'd been caught, I would have spent the rest of my life in jail.'

'What happened?' Jack asked out of politeness. He was getting a little tired of hearing Edgar's amazing adventures.

'I took refuge under the bed of a Russian nun.'

'That must have been quite dangerous for her.'

'I did reward her with a necklace for her troubles.'

'So you gave a nun a stolen necklace?'

'The necklace wasn't stolen. I had just borrowed—'

'Yes,' Mr Doyle cut him off. 'I'm sure.'

Finishing his meal, Mr Doyle turned to Jack. 'Are you sure you want to do this, my boy?' he said. 'It's very risky.'

'I'm doing it,' Jack said. 'Nothing could change my mind.'

'You'll be fine,' Edgar said. 'Just follow my plan and we'll be drinking hot cocoa together in a few hours.'

'What is your plan?' Hiro asked.

'We are now located across the road from the Japanese Museum,' he said. 'Jack will gain access via the roof, navigate to the room containing the Moon Sword and swap it for a copy.'

'Museum authorities won't be fooled by a copy,' Mr Doyle pointed out.

'They won't be fooled *for long*. That's all we'll need. Scarlet will be back with us, safe and sound, by the time the alarm is raised.'

'I assume you've thought this out in detail.'

'I have. As long as Jack follows my plan, he'll be fine. If he doesn't, the next time he sees freedom will be some time after his thirtieth birthday.'

Jack listened intently as Edgar went through the finer details. He gave Jack a map showing him his path.

'There's one final thing,' Edgar said. 'There shouldn't be any guards in the museum.'

'*Shouldn't?*'

'But there might be. I was never able to ascertain whether the building had guards at night or if that were just a rumour.'

Wonderful, Jack thought.

They went to the roof. The night air was cold, a distant rumble rolled across the sky and lightning flashed.

'Please be careful, my boy,' Mr Doyle said.

'I will.'

Hiro took Jack's arm. 'I am sorry,' he said. 'But I cannot stay. I promised my aunt I would buy her some medicine, and the shop is only open at night.'

'That's all right,' Jack said. 'I appreciate everything you've done.'

Hiro bowed to Jack. 'You are very brave,' he said. 'May the gods keep you safe.'

Jack thanked him and took a deep breath.

It's time.

CHAPTER THIRTY-ONE

Edgar swung a piece of rope with a grappling hook attached and launched it twenty feet across the alley where it looped around a chimney. He tied the other end to a hotel chimney and pulled tight.

After Jack put on the backpack, he started across the rope, using a pole for balance. Below him, the city was in full swing, the streets crowded with people and traffic, but he had to ignore all that. He focused on putting one foot before the other and was soon stepping onto the opposite roof.

He dropped the pole and gave the others a wave. *Now for the hard part.*

Jack used a screwdriver to pull out a grille on the

air-conditioning unit. Once he'd lit a candle, he saw it continued down for about twenty feet before branching in two directions.

Attaching another grappling hook to the roof, he lowered himself to the bottom and took the left branch. It was tight in the vent, and he had to slither along on his stomach. He soon reached another vent that looked out onto a display room, filled with Japanese pottery and paintings.

Undoing the screws, Jack gently pulled out the grille and climbed into the room. The museum was as quiet as a cemetery, lit only by tiny gaslights set into the walls.

Replacing the grille, he crept down a wide corridor, passing sections on Geology, Biology and Modern Steam Technology.

He was about to cross a hallway to the Ancient History section when he stopped, straining his ears. Someone was coming.

Jack drew back into a side chamber and took refuge under a cabinet filled with fossils. A guard's steps grew near.

The man entered the room. He said something in Japanese, and Jack's heart almost stopped. He had a dog with him.

Tilting its head, it eyed Jack curiously. Jack didn't dare move a muscle until the man and dog left.

He let out a long breath as the footsteps faded, waiting another five minutes before leaving his hiding spot. Dripping with sweat, Jack's heart was still beating fast.

Crossing to the opposite room, he paused in the doorway. The Moon Sword sat in a glass case on a stone pedestal in the centre.

The glass case wasn't alarmed, but the floor was. Stepping on it would activate an alarm, causing every steam-powered door in the building to lock automatically. The police would arrive and it would be game over.

Jack took out the grappling gun from the backpack and pointed it at the darkened rafter running across the middle of the room.

Phut!

The hook flew over the rafter and fastened. Stepping back a few feet, Jack took a running jump and swung across the room, his feet skimming inches over the floor. His momentum carried him most of the way across, but not far enough. Throwing his body backwards, he increased his rate of swing to reach the display cabinet.

Footsteps approached. Grunting with effort, Jack climbed up the rope to the rafter. Dragging the rope after him, he watched in horror as the guard and dog appeared again. They stood in the doorway, watching.

Did they hear me?

The dog looked up and stared directly at Jack.

Then the guard looked up too.

Jack was frozen with terror. The guard continued to stare, before dropping his gaze and reaching into his pocket. He took out a half-eaten sandwich and started chewing it.

It's too dark up here for him to see me!

The guard finished his meal, whistled to his dog and left.

Jack waited a while longer before dropping the rope, climbing down and resuming his swing across the room. A few minutes later he reached the display case.

Now Jack spotted one last obstacle. The display case was made from a moulded piece of glass with hinges attaching it to the pedestal on one side and a lock at the other. He would need to unlock it while precariously gripping the pedestal with his legs.

Give me something difficult to do.

Having wrapped his legs around the pedestal, Jack had the case unlocked in seconds. He took out the Moon Sword. The ancient weapon had weight, balance and gravitas, unlike the replica. A close examination of the copy would reveal it to be a fraud in seconds, but hopefully that wouldn't happen for several hours.

Relocking the case, he swung back towards the door, tucking the sword into his backpack. He would be close enough to jump to it in seconds.

Just as Jack was about to release the rope, he heard footsteps again.

You've got to be joking.

With one final burst of momentum, he gripped one of the half-open doors and pulled himself onto its top edge, just as the guard and dog reappeared into the doorway.

The guard stared into the chamber, the dog whining and twisting its head, looking straight at Jack.

Go away!

The guard lingered for another minute before moving on, taking the dog with him. The footsteps receded.

Jack hadn't realised he was holding his breath, but now he gasped.

I'm not suited to burglary.

Gently easing himself off the door, he reeled in the hook and rope.

The corridor was deserted. But when he peeped around the corner, he spotted a security guard approaching.

Damn.

Jack turned back the way he had come and sprinted to the opposite corner. Another guard was coming.

I'm trapped!

Jack had to create a diversion—but what? Nothing in the backpack would help. Reaching into his pockets, he pulled out a slingshot and a rock. Peeping around the corner, he saw the nearest guard had paused to look in a room filled with ancient tapestries.

Using the slingshot, Jack fired the rock past the man. As it bounced down the hall, the guard spun about at the sound and raced after it.

Jack used the opportunity to scamper into the tapestry room. A moment later, a second guard passed the room. The men began talking. One had the rock in his hand, confused. Jack scampered down the hallway.

I'll be fine once I'm around the corner, he thought. *Just a few more—*

One of the guards yelled.

No!

The guards began to give chase. Dogs started barking.

I've got to get back to the vent. Once there, Jack stood a chance of escaping.

He rounded a corner—and came face to face with a guard and his dog.

The guard drew a baton, but Jack came in low with a sweeping kick, knocking him to the floor. His dog lunged at Jack, grabbing his coat, but somehow Jack managed to pull away.

He ran. The entire museum had come to life. An alarm bell shrilled. A dog chased him.

Jack dragged a piece of steak from the backpack and tossed it behind. Glancing back, he saw the dog had stopped to eat it.

Good thinking, Mr Doyle.

But now guards were appearing from all directions. Jack raced down another hallway, lost.

Where is the exit?

His eyes narrowed on a room containing pots and ancient paintings.

There it is!

He charged into the room, but half-a-dozen guards were almost on him, one yelling orders in Japanese.

Jack spun around to face them. The men didn't have guns, but they had batons. He might be able to fight off one or two, but not all of them.

This is hopeless, he thought. *I can't escape.*

CHAPTER THIRTY-TWO

The guards started towards him—and then stopped, their eyes widening in surprise. A sound came from behind and Jack turned to see the red ninja, slipping nimbly from the vent like a cat. She gave him a small nod, a smile in her eyes.

I know those eyes, Jack thought. *But from where?*

One of the guards charged, baton raised, but the red ninja went low, sweeping the guard's legs from under him. She grabbed his baton and flung it at another guard's knee, who immediately fell, howling. Next, she hurled throwing stars at the feet of the remaining guards and they all dropped to the ground in agony.

Effortlessly, the red ninja lifted Jack to the vent.

Scrambling inside, he followed it to where it angled upwards, the ninja close behind. Raised voices came from the room as the alarm continued to ring.

Jack and the ninja reached the roof.

'Thank you,' he breathed. 'How will I ever repay you?'

The red ninja simply shook her head.

Swallowing, Jack said, 'But now they will check the museum and realise I stole the Moon Sword.'

The red ninja reached back and, producing a rolled up painting, showed it to Jack. He understood her plan.

They'll think our goal was to steal the painting. It'll be hours before they realise the Moon Sword is also gone.

She pointed to the rope leading to the hotel. Jack crossed it in seconds, falling into Mr Doyle's arms.

'Jack!'

'The red ninja saved me!' Jack said.

'I know, Jack,' Mr Doyle said. 'We saw her.'

They gazed back at the museum roof, but she was already gone.

Grabbing their gear, Jack and Mr Doyle returned to their hotel room. There wasn't a moment to waste. Edgar took the backpack downstairs and dropped it into a side alley.

'No doubt the police will find it and assume the thief has escaped in a vehicle,' he said when he returned.

'You've obviously thought this through,' Mr Doyle muttered.

They glanced out the window. The streets were

filled with noisy people and police vehicles arriving. Reporters turned up to interview museum officials, while photographers set up cameras.

'I wouldn't have escaped if not for the ninja,' Jack said.

'We owe her a great deal,' Mr Doyle agreed.

Edgar spoke up. 'I suggest we get a few hours sleep,' he said. 'We'll leave early in the morning for Fujita's tower.'

The next morning, they woke just after dawn. As they were heading out the door, Edgar proudly wielded the Moon Sword.

'This is a work of art,' he said. 'The best Japanese swords were made by master swordmakers who folded the hot metal hundreds of times to make them stronger.'

'Will it fool Fujita?' Jack asked.

'It should,' Edgar said. 'I've checked the early edition of the paper and found no mention of its theft. The museum officials should be fooled for some time.'

'You sound pretty confident.'

Edgar smiled. 'I used a similar tactic at the Monet Museum some years back,' he said. 'There was a lovely watercolour that I swapped for a copy.'

'And it fooled them?'

Leaning close to Jack, he said, 'To this day.'

Edgar wrapped the sword in a piece of cloth, grabbed another bag and they headed to the roof. Hiro was waiting. Another storm was in progress. Lightning flashed across the sky.

The dragonfly struggled as it took off against the gusty winds.

Gaining altitude, Jack said to Hiro, 'Are you sure you'll be able to land on the tower?'

'With difficulty,' he said.

'I wonder if Fujita will keep his word.'

'I have my doubts,' Hiro admitted.

'We have a backup plan,' Edgar said.

His bag contained four small backpacks made of something that looked like a spider web.

'What are they?' he asked.

'Parachutes,' Edgar said. 'I suggest we all wear them. They're small enough to fit under your clothing.'

Mr Doyle raised an eyebrow. 'You think we might need to jump off the building?' he asked.

'Simply a precaution.'

Jack put the parachute on under his coat.

The wind tore at the dragonfly, throwing it about like a cork on a restless sea. The sky had turned leaden with rain falling in big, gusty sprays. A distant rumble echoed across Tokyo.

'There it is,' Edgar said, pointing to a tower rearing from the mist.

Mr Doyle leant closer to the window. 'Good Lord!' he exclaimed.

The rooftop was as before: half Fujita's residence, the other half a rooftop garden and landing pad. Now two figures stood in the torrential rain on the ledge at the far side of the garden. One was Scarlet, handcuffed.

The other was Dr Livanov, who held a knife to Scarlet's throat.

'Those monsters!' Mr Doyle muttered, clenching his fists. 'I swear, if they've harmed her...'

'Easy,' Edgar muttered, clenching his brother's arm. 'We must keep our wits about us. Emotion will only lead us astray.'

Hiro made a loop around the penthouse, fighting against the wind before landing the dragonfly. Jack, Edgar and Mr Doyle climbed out while Hiro remained at the controls. Jack peered at Scarlet. She was drenched by the pouring rain, but otherwise appeared unharmed. She gave him a quick nod.

Fujita appeared from the apartment.

'We have what you want,' Mr Doyle called. 'We have brought you the Kusanagi sword.'

'Give it to me,' Fujita ordered.

Edgar lifted the sword high. Lightning flashed, and for one brief moment, Jack wondered if it might strike the sword and kill them all.

'Not until Scarlet is safe,' Mr Doyle said.

But the weapon had transfixed Fujita. Rousing himself, he nodded to Livanov, who started along the ledge, keeping a firm grip on Scarlet's arm.

'Now the sword,' Fujita said.

Mr Doyle's eyes settled on the weapon. Though his jaw was clenched, the detective remained silent as Edgar crossed to Fujita. The crime boss frowned, snatching the sword from him.

'No!' he exclaimed. 'This is a fake!'

Jack ran towards Scarlet. At the same moment, one of the blinds went up in the apartment, revealing a man with a machine gun. Mr Doyle produced his gun and fired, but the assassin ducked as the window exploded. A hail of bullets spat into the brickwork around Jack as he weaved through the garden.

Scarlet struggled against Livanov, but the doctor drew back a fist, slamming her in the face. Swooning, Scarlet teetered on the ledge as Jack expelled an extra burst of speed.

Almost there, he thought. *Just a few more seconds.*

But he was too late. Livanov gave Jack a sick smile as she pushed Scarlet over the edge.

'No!' Jack screamed.

Livanov ran at Jack, but he ducked, slamming a fist into her nose. She staggered backwards, her foot slipping over the edge. She teetered for a moment before she fell, screaming.

Without hesitation, Jack jumped off the building too. *I have to save Scarlet.* She was already far below, the wind pulling her away from the tower.

Jack tucked in his arms and legs to reduce wind resistance.

Fly, he told himself. *Like a bird.*

Spreading his arms, he tilted his body and the wind caught him, slowing his descent. The tower raced past, a blur in the corner of his vision as he and Scarlet fell through low-lying clouds. One of Scarlet's arms moved.

Her eyes shuttered open, and she screamed.

Jack was still twenty feet above her. Screaming her name, his voice was whipped away by the wind, but then her eyes focused on him in disbelief. He pulled his limbs in and dropped another ten feet, before spreading out again like a bird.

Scarlet reached out to him as Jack stretched with all his might.

Only five feet separated them.

Four. Three. Two.

Their fingers touched.

She grabbed his hand, and they drew close. Wrapping his body around her, Jack reached for the cord and pulled it.

CHAPTER THIRTY-THREE

'That was close,' Jack said.

Half a day had passed and they were now sitting back in their hotel next to the museum. Mr Doyle, Edgar and Hiro had escaped the battle on the rooftop of Fujita's tower. Mr Doyle had killed the man inside with the machine gun, but not before Edgar had received a flesh wound. Fujita had escaped.

'I thought we were finished,' Scarlet said. 'I didn't know you had a parachute.'

'I didn't know if it would work,' Jack replied.

Edgar smiled. 'I'm told the parachutes are the best ever developed,' he said. 'Their success rate is as high as seventy per cent.'

'*Seventy per cent?*'

The storm had eased. Rain splashed against the window as they drank their tea and thought about the day's events. Mr Doyle sat quietly opposite his brother. The detective had said little since Hiro had collected them from the base of Fujita's tower. Edgar continued to prattle on in his usual gregarious manner.

'There's always risks,' Edgar was saying. 'I've been in some pretty tough situations over the years, but you know what makes the difference?'

'What?' Mr Doyle said.

'The friends at your side. You know what the Bard said about friends? *Grapple them unto thy soul with hoops of steel.*'

Mr Doyle nodded slowly. 'You're right,' he said. 'I know I'm a lucky man. More lucky than I deserve. I lost my son in the war, but I got him back. How many people can say that?'

'Not many,' Edgar agreed.

'And I'm blessed to have Jack and Scarlet in my life,' Mr Doyle said, turning to them. 'My wife and I would have been the luckiest parents in the world to have children one-tenth as wonderful as you.'

Scarlet wiped a tear away as Jack swallowed hard.

'Thank you, Mr Doyle,' he said.

'Of course,' Mr Doyle continued, 'a man can't have everything.' The detective's face hardened. 'We can't pick our family, can we? Especially when your brother is a rogue and a criminal.'

The smile on Edgar's face faltered. 'But that's all water under the bridge now,' he said. 'As the Bard said—'

'Shut up,' Mr Doyle said, his face now white with fury. 'Where is it?'

'Where's...what?'

'The Moon Sword.'

'Why...' Edgar appeared bewildered. 'Back at Fujita's tower. We left it behind as we made our getaway.'

'It never made it to Fujita's tower,' Mr Doyle said. 'So I'll ask you again—where is the Moon Sword?'

'Mr Doyle,' Jack said. 'We took the sword to the tower in exchange for Scarlet.'

'No, we took *a* sword to the tower. The sword that Edgar handed Fujita wasn't the Moon Sword. It was a fake.'

'But I stole it from the Japanese Museum.'

'You did indeed,' Mr Doyle said. 'But Edgar couldn't bear to part with it.' He turned to his brother. 'Could you? Was that your plan all along? For Jack to steal the sword so that you would switch it with a replica? Do you realise what you did? Your greed endangered Scarlet's life. She could have been killed because of your stupidity!'

'No, I—'

'At least have the courage to admit it!'

Edgar's mouth fell open as he looked at them helplessly.

'I'm sorry,' he stammered. 'It's true. It's all true.'

Now Jack understood the look on Mr Doyle's face

as Edgar handed the sword to Fujita. He had immediately recognised it as a fake.

'I don't know why I did it,' Edgar said. 'I don't know why I do a lot of things. I suppose I'm a small man. Ignatius has always been the big man in our family, the successful one. Smarter. Driven. A man to be admired.'

The room was completely silent except for the rain and the sounds of the city. A dragonfly buzzed overhead.

'I'm sorry,' Edgar said. 'I never meant—Watch out!'

He threw himself at Mr Doyle as a hail of bullets smashed through the window. The roar of an engine became deafeningly loud, then the wall exploded inwards, sending debris flying.

A section of ceiling collapsed, narrowly missing Jack. He crawled out from under the devastation and saw a mechanical dragonfly, hovering above. Twice the size of its biological counterpart, its wings moved almost too fast for the eye to see. Its body was armoured with machine guns and rocket launchers were set into the head. Its whine was ear-splitting.

Jack screamed as the guns came to life.

Rat-atat-atat!

Bullets raked the walls, and plaster and timber spat in all directions.

'Come on!' Scarlet screamed.

But Jack couldn't move. The sound of the gunfire had frozen him to the spot. Then he felt a hand at his shoulder. It was Hiro, and he proceeded to drag Jack and Scarlet from the room.

'Mr Doyle!' Jack cried, coming to his senses.

'Right behind us,' Hiro grunted.

Mr Doyle helped Edgar from the room. They staggered down the hall as another explosion came from behind, completely destroying their apartment.

'What's going on?' Jack asked, bewildered. 'Is it Fujita?'

'No,' Mr Doyle said. He had his arm around Edgar. 'The men at the controls are dressed in trench coats.'

Nazis.

More rockets were fired at the building as they lurched down the stairs. Alarm bells rang as people abandoned the hotel. Racing into the street, Jack saw the mechanical dragonfly pull back from the building. Its rocket launchers locked into place.

'Run!' Mr Doyle cried.

Jack didn't need any urging, but there was no time for thought, no time for reasoning, no time to make any kind of plan. The building gave an ominous groan. People screamed. The rocket launchers fired.

A giant shadow passed over him, and then—nothing.

When he next opened his eyes, Jack realised he was buried under rubble. He could hardly breathe. Dust was up his nose and down his throat.

Pushing at a piece of wood, Jack eventually broke free of the debris.

The hotel had collapsed. Hiro and Scarlet were further down the street, half-buried under bricks and broken timber, not moving.

Mr Doyle was trying to drag Edgar clear.

The dragonfly started to swing towards the street. The machine guns locked into position.

We'll never get away in time, Jack thought. *If only I had a weapon—*

His eyes settled on the long, silver case, lying in the debris—the Kusanagi sword was supposed to lie within, but all it held was that useless handle.

But what had the old man in the garden said?

There is a gap between knowing and science.

Jack dragged himself across the debris.

The path will find you.

He reached the sword case. Did he truly believe in the power of the Kusanagi sword?

The whine of the dragonfly was deafening as Jack opened the case. He took out the handle and lifted it over his head.

The dragonfly now swept towards him and Jack saw the machine gun aim at his chest.

Whack!

The fist that slammed into the side of Jack's face drove him to the ground. The handle clattered away from him. Dazed, he struggled to reach for it, but a boot slammed down, crushing his hand. He looked up to see Anton Drexler grinning at him.

'You have done well,' the Nazi said, as the dragonfly pulled away. 'We came here to finish off you and your mentor. Retrieving the sword—even this fragment—is a bonus!' Laughing, he picked up the handle. 'Now we'll see what power the sword contains—if any!'

Grinning down at Jack, Drexler lifted the sword overhead. 'You see?' he said. 'It is nothing! Just a—' The smile faded from his face. 'What?'

The handle began to glow.

'No,' Drexler grunted. 'What is happening?'

He tried releasing the sword, but it was as if it was glued to his hand. Smoke began pouring from his fist as orange flames slid down his arm.

'No!' he screamed. 'I can't let go! It's attached to me!'

The flame spread across Drexler's body, drowning him in fire. The Nazi continued to scream, but his cries were lost in the fiery blast. He glowed as bright as the sun before he was pulverised and the handle clattered to the ground.

Slowly, Jack became aware of the rain, the debris and the dozens of fires that continued to burn. A distant sound cut through the downpour from above.

Cra-ack!

The wall next to Jack had started to move. It was collapsing—on him!

He ran, but it was already too late. The bricks and mortar slammed into him, burying his legs.

Gasping with pain, he raised his head to see the mechanical dragonfly had started to turn. It began down the street towards him.

I've got to get out of here, Jack thought. *But I can't move!*

Then a figure broke from a doorway. The red ninja!

She raced towards Jack, desperately pulling debris away. A hail of bullets slammed into the roadwork, racing towards Jack and the ninja. She dragged him towards a doorway as the gunfire reached them.

'Aaarrgh!' she cried as she fell, screaming.

Jack pulled the red ninja clear as her upper arm darkened with blood. Taking out a handkerchief, Jack started bandaging her arm. As he did, her mask slipped away—revealing her face.

'No,' Jack gasped. 'It's not possible.'

'But it is.' The familiar face of Hiro looked back up at him. 'It seems you have discovered my little secret.'

'But you're male!' Jack said.

'No,' Hiro said. 'I am not.'

Dressed in a suit, Hiro had always resembled a young man, but now it was as if a curtain had been removed from Jack's eyes. And not only was Hiro female—she was also the red ninja.

'Why...?' Jack started.

'There isn't time to discuss this,' Hiro said. 'You must save the others.'

'How can I do that?'

But he already knew how. Gently releasing Hiro, Jack raced back into the street where the sword handle lay in the debris. The dragonfly had already begun another run. Jack lifted the handle high as the mechanical dragonfly bore down, the machine guns aimed directly at him.

Then a blast of wind, so powerful that it almost

lifted Jack into the air, burst down the alley from behind. Howling like an avenging spirit, it blocked out all sound as it slammed into the dragonfly, throwing it sideways.

The pilot struggled to control the vessel, but then one wing clipped a wall. Going to full power, the dragonfly fought to climb from the alley as another gust of wind smashed into it. The vessel crashed into a building before it cartwheeled towards the ground and exploded.

The rain continued to fall as Jack lowered the sword.

'Jack?'

Scarlet was climbing over the rubble towards him. He threw himself into her arms. Hiro appeared from a building, dressed in his normal clothing, gripping his arm. Together, they all scrambled over the devastation to Mr Doyle and his brother.

The detective had Edgar in his arms. 'Just hold on,' Mr Doyle was saying. 'Help will be here soon.'

The front of Edgar's shirt was drenched with blood.

'I don't want to let you down, old chap,' Edgar said. 'Not again.'

'You couldn't let me down,' Mr Doyle said, taking Edgar's hand. 'You're my brother.'

'But you know what the Bard said: *All that lives must die, passing through nature to eternity.*' He coughed, his lips red. 'You remember the safe house I visited? There's a few items I borrowed that probably need returning.'

'Oh Edgar...'

'Don't fret, Ignatius. I'll be joining mother and father for tea.'

'Hang on. Just a while longer.'

Edgar's eyes focused on Jack. 'What about that sword?' he said. 'I always knew it had magic.'

Jack nodded. He started to speak, but Edgar was beyond hearing. The rain tumbled down, fires burned and people wailed. And the wind howled, eternally.

CHAPTER THIRTY-FOUR

'Our families are often not what we want,' Mr Doyle said. 'Mothers and fathers don't live up to expectations. Children take paths against their parents' wishes.' He paused. 'Brothers are not what you want them to be.'

A week had passed since Edgar's death. Jack, Scarlet and Mr Doyle were back home in London, and Gloria was finally bringing her files up to date.

'My brother was a rogue, a criminal and a conman,' Mr Doyle said as Gloria handed out cups of tea.

'And he was your brother,' Jack said.

Mr Doyle nodded sadly. 'And he was my brother.'

'So,' Gloria said, 'Anna Livanov was working for the Metalists?'

'We believe she was in their employment for some time,' Mr Doyle said. 'They paid her off to bring down the Darwinist League. She caused the explosion on the space steamer, *Katsu*, on the way to Japan. A specially designed escape pod was supposed to enable her to get away. When that failed, she murdered Dr Hodder, hoping the symposium would be cancelled, but it wasn't. Later, she did her best to destroy Mizu City. Once again, she had a way out: an additional jellysuit that nobody knew about.'

'And the Nazis?'

'They were involved in the search for the Kusanagi sword long before we arrived in Japan. When they realised Edgar was following a trail of maps, they started trailing him. When he went missing, they didn't know what to do.'

'Until we arrived,' Jack said. 'So they started following us.'

'They tried stealing pieces of the map on several occasions,' Scarlet added, 'but without success. It seems Drexler had given up on ever finding the sword when the mechanical dragonfly attacked us at the hotel. Of course, that didn't end well for him.'

'And what about Fujita?' Gloria asked. 'Has he escaped prison?'

'Not at all,' Mr Doyle said. 'A few days after the devastation at the hotel, he was arrested for a minor offence by police.'

'A strange coincidence.'

'It wasn't a coincidence at all,' Jack said. 'Mr Doyle

had filed a full report on him.'

'By then, they already had him under twenty-four-hour surveillance. The robot dragon had killed the son of a police chief who had previously worked for Fujita, and the tide was turning against him. The police searched the boot of his steamcar and found both the Moon Sword and a priceless painting, both recently stolen from the Japanese museum.'

'Really?' Gloria raised an eyebrow. 'Was that your doing?'

'Not at all.'

'So how did the sword and the painting end up in Fujita's car?'

Jack leant forward. 'There is really only one possible explanation,' he said. 'The red ninja.'

'Goodness,' Gloria said. 'I'm glad she's on our side. I suppose we'll never know her true identity?'

Mr Doyle stared at Jack as if he could see right through him.

'Jack?' Mr Doyle said. 'Do you wish to enlighten us?'

Jack frowned. 'Something tells me you already know,' he said.

'That Hiro was the red ninja all along?'

'*What*?' Scarlet shrieked.

'Hiro didn't swear me to secrecy,' Jack said. 'But it's best if the knowledge doesn't leave this room.'

Gloria closed her file.

Jack explained how he had discovered Hiro's other identity.

'After we took Hiro to the hospital, she told me Fujita was responsible for both the death of her parents and her uncle. She had sworn she would avenge their deaths.'

'But how did she become a ninja?' Gloria asked. 'Especially once her uncle was killed?'

'Well,' Jack said. 'She still had an aunt.'

'She was trained by her aunt?'

Jack shrugged. 'The best way to keep a secret is to make it seem completely unlikely,' Jack said. 'And a long tradition of female ninjas training other female ninjas is about as unlikely as you can get.'

'Come to think of it,' Scarlet said. 'He—I mean—*she* did slip away a lot.'

'Hiro disappeared before every appearance of the red ninja: at the fort, the museum, Fujita's tower.' Jack turned to Mr Doyle. 'But how did you already know?'

'How did I know?' Mr Doyle said, pulling a lump of cheese from his pocket. 'In that respect, it was reminiscent of a case involving a stolen garden gnome, a singing duck and—'

'Mr Doyle!'

'Oh, of course.' He returned the cheese to his pocket. 'You recall when Hiro was knocked unconscious during our rescue of Edgar from Fujita's tower? And I tended to his, rather *her*, wounds?'

'Yes.'

'Well…Hiro was lumpy in all the wrong places. Putting two and two together, I realised he was a she.

That, in conjunction with his opportune disappearances, cemented it for me.'

Jack nodded, remembering the red ninja at the museum. 'I knew her eyes looked familiar,' he said. 'It was because they were Hiro's.'

'And the Kusanagi sword?' Gloria asked.

Mr Doyle reddened. 'There are two aspects to this investigation that will never be fully explained,' he said. 'Jack and Scarlet both tell me the sword created a mighty wind that destroyed the dragonfly. I cannot confirm that as I was caring for Edgar at the time. There was a wind, certainly, but I believe it was the storm.'

'And you?' Gloria asked Jack and Scarlet.

'There was a massive wind,' Scarlet said. 'The most powerful breeze I've ever encountered.'

'Jack?'

He smiled. As the wind had swept down the street towards the dragonfly, Jack recalled looking up at the handle. For as long as he lived, he knew he would always remember the glowing sword rising from it, shimmering as if made from hot glass.

'Jack?' Mr Doyle ventured.

'Belief is a powerful thing,' Jack said. 'That's all I'll say.'

'You said there were two aspects,' Gloria said to Mr Doyle. 'What was the second?'

Mr Doyle sighed. 'I'm sure there's a logical explanation,' he said. 'We went in search of the garden where Hikaru Satou approached us.'

'And?'

'There was a memorial stone in his honour,' Mr Doyle said. 'He has been dead for nine years.'

Jack shivered. *Ghosts?* How was such a thing possible? But if there was one thing he had learnt during his time with Mr Doyle, the world was a stranger place than anyone could imagine.

'This case has it all,' Gloria said. 'Magical swords, ghosts, ninjas. Whatever will be next?'

Almost as if in response, a ring came from the front office. When Gloria returned, she looked puzzled.

'There's a man,' she said. 'He refuses to give his name.'

A figure appeared behind her. 'Herr Doyle and his brats may already know me,' he said. 'We met, briefly, some time ago.'

Jack stared at the man. He *had* seen him once before, during his first adventure with Mr Doyle. This man had been one of the Nazis responsible for kidnapping Scarlet and her father.

'You're Adolf Hitler,' Mr Doyle said. 'One of Drexler's henchmen.'

'Now that Drexler is dead,' Hitler said, 'I lead the party.'

'What do you want?'

'To congratulate you, of course,' Hitler said. 'It is in the newspapers that the Kusanagi sword has been recovered, and returned to the Japanese government. No doubt Japan will be a loyal ally to England in the future.'

'And?'

'England will need its allies. A war is coming and a reckoning will be paid.'

'The German people will not follow a maniac like you.'

'They may not need to. Many men have led nations, but none have ruled a world. I intend to be the first.'

'You're insane.'

'They said that about Napoleon too.'

'Why are you here?' Jack asked.

'I have a long memory,' Hitler said. 'I will not forget you, Herr Doyle, or your brats. The day will come when you will regret standing against us.' He gave them one final twisted smile. 'I wish you good day.'

After he had left, Gloria locked the front door. 'What a horrible creature,' she said.

'People are always looking for leaders,' Mr Doyle said, glumly. 'Sometimes the bad ones are all too easy to find.'

Jack fell back in his seat, his heart pounding, his hands shaking. His eyes went from Gloria to Scarlet and, finally, Mr Doyle.

'Jack?' Mr Doyle said. 'What is it?'

He looked at his shaking hands as if they didn't belong to him. 'Believe it or not,' Jack said. 'I'm afraid.'

'Afraid?' Scarlet said. 'Jack, you've jumped off towers, fought off sharks, battled evildoers, and faced death more times than Brinkie Buckeridge. What can you possibly be afraid of?'

It took Jack a moment to find the words. 'I think I'm afraid of the future,' he said. 'Hitler says there's going to be another war, and maybe there will be. Millions of people will die if there is. The Hot Earth Accord has been signed, meaning that Biomechanics will completely change the way we live. It's all so...big.' He spread his arms. 'What are we going to do?'

Mr Doyle didn't speak for a moment. Then he said, 'Come to the balcony.'

They followed him to the other end of the apartment where they could see the landscape of London. Here, they watched the shifting seas of smoke and fog creasing the horizon as airships cut silent paths across the skyline.

The London Metrotower, a city in itself, speared upwards to the edge of space. At the top, people were planning to get to the moon, while others dreamt of going even further.

Jack peered down at the steamcars chugging along crowded Bee Street. Further down the block vehicles disappeared into a cloud of steam and fog, as though disappearing into the past itself.

The locket of his parents, and the compass, jiggled in his pocket, a reminder that the past was always there, no matter how far he went into the future.

Jack looked into Gloria's face. It seemed strange that he had known her for less than a year, yet she had already become like a mother to him. How else could you describe the person who cooked your meals, bandaged your wounds and hugged away your pains?

His eyes met Scarlet. As she smiled, he hesitantly took her hand. It seemed impossible that there had ever been a time when he had not known her. Jack hoped she would always be the most wonderful friend he would ever know—or maybe, in the future, something more…

Finally, his eyes moved to Mr Doyle's face. The detective was strange, brilliant and kind, and he had guided Jack, taught him and given him opportunities where there had been none.

Wasn't that what a father did?

Jack's mind wandered back to the conclusion of their first adventure. He remembered Mr Doyle had proposed a toast.

To family.

This was where Jack was now. With his family.

Mr Doyle pointed to a man and woman holding the hands of a little boy, as they strolled along Bee street.

'You asked what we will do, Jack,' Mr Doyle said. 'Look at those people, a man and woman with dreams of the future. Dreams for themselves. Dreams for their son. They're not prime ministers or leaders of industry or crime bosses. They're ordinary people united by love.'

He pulled Jack, Scarlet and Gloria close to him.

'We'll do everything we can to make the world a better place. And we'll believe in love.'

**OVERNEWTON ANGLICAN
COMMUNITY COLLEGE
LIBRARY**